Hurst and Blackett, limited

Virginia Tennant

Vol. I

Hurst and Blackett, limited

Virginia Tennant
Vol. I

ISBN/EAN: 9783337247805

Printed in Europe, USA, Canada, Australia, Japan

Cover: Foto ©Andreas Hilbeck / pixelio.de

More available books at **www.hansebooks.com**

BY THE AUTHOR OF

"CHRISTINA NORTH," "A GOLDEN BAR,"
"BETWIXT MY LOVE AND ME,"
ETC., ETC.

' Where lies the land to which the ship would go?
Far, far ahead, is all her seamen know.
And where the land she travels from?   Away.
Far, far behind is all that they can say.'

IN TWO VOLUMES.

VOL. I.

LONDON:
HURST AND BLACKETT, LIMITED,
13, GREAT MARLBOROUGH STREET.
1888.

VIRGINIA TENNANT.

CHAPTER I.

IT was a wild night. Outside the harbour the sea was throwing up angry crests of foam, and the wind blew in the sudden and opposing gusts which precede a tempest; whilst round about the pier the water, as it beat with a sullen crash, looked black in the gathering twilight. But no sound or presage of the coming storm had penetrated the well-curtained rooms of the large hotel which stood in the shelter of the cliff, though at the distance of but a few hundred yards from the shore.

Within one of its best apartments the

lamps were already lighted, and, though it was early in October, a fire was blazing on the hearth, giving an air of comfort to the otherwise comfortless room, with its heavy, handsome, scanty furniture. A half-opened travelling-bag was upon the floor, a fur cloak was thrown across a chair; the cloth and glasses with an untouched dessert were still upon the table.

There were two persons in the room: a handsome man barely above middle-age, who, with his chair pushed back, leaned one arm still upon the table, while the other was passed round the shoulders of a girl who sat on a low stool at his feet. Her head, with its low masses of brown hair, rested against his knees, but her eyes were fixedly bent upon the dancing flames.

'You are crying, Virginia,' he said, in a tone of gentle reproof. 'You told me this morning that there should be no tears, and you are crying already.'

'I am not;' yet she saw the fire, at

which she was staring, through a mist. 'I am not crying; but I hate war and Egypt and the Soudan.'

'And soldiers, even though your father is one?' asked Colonel Tennant, smiling. 'If I were you, I would not hate the inevitable. It is not worth while.'

'If it is not worth while to hate, it is still worse to love.'

She lifted her head as she spoke, and sat upright with her hands clasped round her knees. Some sudden resentment against life, which at this moment dealt so hardly with her, had dried the unshed tears in her blue eyes.

'Yes, it is still worse to love,' he repeated, 'only one cannot avoid it, and unfortunately when one loves it is always the inevitable.'

His hand still rested upon her soft hair, but as he spoke he was looking absently back into the past.

She sat still as if pondering the question, and there was a short silence. Outside in the darkness there was the crash of breaking surf upon the shingle, and a church clock struck the hour in slow, ponderous strokes. Each one fell with a dull presentiment of coming anguish upon the girl's heart. So remorselessly would be taken from her the few short hours before the moment of parting which was so surely drawing near. She glanced at the clock upon the mantelpiece, and looked away again quickly.

'How old are you?' asked Colonel Tennant, suddenly, with an apparently unconnected change of ideas.

'I was twenty on my last birthday, papa.' She looked a little surprised.

'Twenty! The years have passed quickly.'

'Do you think so? I should say, on the contrary, that the time has been like a summer's day, beautiful but *long*. It seems to me to be a life-time since I was a child, a year since we came to England. Papa, now that you must leave me, why cannot I go back to La Vallière with Mademoiselle Joseph? If I could be happy without you, I could be happy there.'

Her father put that question aside, and only replied to it by another.

'You have often been happy without me before. Do you think that you know how to be unhappy?'

'I am learning. You are teaching me.'

'The last lesson that I wish you to learn! Do not say that, my child; you must try to be happy without me. It is impossible to let you go back to the solitude of La Vallière. It is time that you should make acquaintance with your relatives, and see something of the world. Your aunt has promised me to watch over you, and you will have a country life in England which at your age was my idea of an earthly paradise. To be sure,' regretfully, 'you cannot shoot and fish, but you will have pursuits and interests of your own. Above all, you will have companions of your own age.'

He stopped suddenly. After all, it was not easy to play the part of a comforter when he felt himself in as great need of consolation as his daughter. He had an unreasonable fear of the unknown dangers which might be awaiting her. She had been brought up in what might now prove to have been an unhealthy seclusion, and she was about to be left, who could say for how long, in the care of those who, though relations, were yet strangers. He knew so little of them that he could form but a faint idea of what their conduct would be towards his motherless girl. And yet he passed his hand fondly over the fair head resting against his knees, and said to himself that Virginia would surely win her way amongst them.

'You will try to make friends of your cousins?' he asked, a little wistfully.

'I shall be sure to like them,' she answered, with a confidence born of ignorance. 'I have seen very few people that I dislike. And, even if I did not like them, it would not matter very much, as it will be for a short time only that I shall be with them.'

'Why a short time?' The question escaped him unawares.

'Why! because you are so soon coming back again;' but an uninvited dread had crept into her voice. 'You said that you should soon come back.'

'Yes—of course—of course,' he answered, hastily; but, reaching backward to look in his face, she saw the cloud which had come over it.

'Promise me that it shall be soon,' she cried, and flung her arms about his knees. And he knew that he could not promise to come back either soon or late. For the first time he was starting upon active service with a heavy heart. He said to himself that it was a superstition, an absurdity, but when he parted with Virginia it would be to him as if they were not to meet again on this side of the grave; he would stand as it were at his own death-bed, and she must never know it.

'I am not commander-in-chief,' he answered, lightly, 'but certainly I have every prospect of being back shortly. Consider, Virginia; be reasonable. I have often left you for a longer time, and for a greater distance, and you have not found it so hard to part from me.'

'It is because I am afraid this time, papa,' she said, in a low voice. 'I cannot tell why it is that I am afraid.'

'Then do not spoil our last evening together with unreasonable terrors.' He turned to the table and poured himself out a glass of wine. 'To our happy meeting again,' he said, smiling as he lifted it to his lips. The girl too forced a smile; and then, as if anxious to turn to another subject, she asked:

'Now tell me something about my cousins, papa.'

'That is not easy. I am afraid my knowledge is somewhat limited. Emmeline has always been more or less of an invalid. I believe she is six or seven years your senior. Hartley is younger, and then there is a schoolboy not more than fourteen or fifteen, I imagine.'

'I believe! I imagine! is that all you can say of your nearest relations?'

'I wish now for your sake I could say more,' said Colonel Tennant, gravely. 'Then I should not be leaving you amongst strangers.'

'Do not you think that they will be certain to like me?' and the girl laughed a little. 'I am not afraid. Besides, I shall always have Mademoiselle Joseph.'

'Then you know,' continued Colonel Tennant, 'Mr. Stansfield's son by his first wife still lives in the house. He looks after the property; it is fortunate that your aunt has him at hand.'

'I wonder if she thinks so,' observed Virginia, 'yet a stepson is not like a step-daughter, bound to hate his father's widow.'

'Indeed, I should hope not. Yet if you should find that any ill-feeling exists . . .'

'I will be sure to take the part of the oppressed, papa.'

'Take no one's part,' he said, sighing involuntarily ; 'a volunteer is sure to do more harm than good, and will please neither of the belligerents. Your little hands,' kissing those he held, 'were meant to make peace, not war.'

A silence fell upon them. They were both conscious of having carried on a con-versation in the endeavour if possible to hide by commonplace words the deepening oppression of anticipated pain.

Suddenly the girl half raised herself, and,

putting her arms about his neck, she hid
her face upon his shoulder. It seemed as
if for the moment his self-control too had
given way. He pressed her closer in his
arms and kissed her hair, her fair brow, her
half-averted cheek.

'You are worn out with your journey,
my sweet one,' he whispered; ' you must
sleep to-night, or you will not be fit to say
good-bye to me to-morrow. You know you
have promised to " smile me adieu," and
you must try to rest to-night. I have
letters to write, and I ought to be at work
now. Let Mademoiselle Joseph stay with
you until you are asleep. Good-night,
Good-night.'

He kissed her once more, and put her
gently away from him. She made no
resistance; perhaps she felt that her powers
of endurance were at an end. She walked
along the passage with her head bent
down, and would certainly have failed to
find her own room if Mademoiselle Joseph

had not been watching for her at the door.

'That is right; come, come in, my poor child,' cried that good-hearted woman, pushing forward a big arm-chair. 'You have left the colonel to his letters! That is best. You will sleep and regain courage.'

'I cannot let him go: I cannot!'

Virginia had sunk trembling into a chair; the tears were running down her pale cheeks.

'As long as one is in this world one must part,' observed Mademoiselle Joseph, sententiously. 'And it is generally with that which one loves the best.'

But Virginia hardly heard her. Worn out in body, her mind could grasp only the one idea, and she was absolutely indifferent to everything else. She let Mademoiselle Joseph assist her to undress, but she gave her no response. For a while she lay exhausted by her tears, watching the shadows on the wall and the old Frenchwoman's tall, angular figure in the chair at the foot of the bed; then the objects became obscured and confused, the vine-leaves on the paper twisted themselves about Mademoiselle Joseph's head, she was on the sea and her bed was tossing upon the waves, she heard their murmur in her ears, and at last she slept.

'It is well,' cried Mademoiselle Joseph, rising cautiously upon tiptoe to look at her. 'I was right; sorrow always sleeps. It is a merciful provision of nature.'

She quitted the room, softly shutting the door behind her, and was slipping along the passage to regain her own apartment when Colonel Tennant's voice arrested her.

'I am waiting to speak to you, mademoiselle, if you will kindly spare me a few minutes.'

He stood on the threshold of the sitting-room holding the door open for her to enter. His handsome face was pale and worn, and a deep dejection was manifest beneath his soldierly bearing. He drew forward a chair for the governess, but remained standing, and for a minute or two kept silence as if he found a difficulty in opening the subject upon which he desired to speak.

'I wished to make one or two matters plain to you before we part, mademoiselle,' he said at last. 'I have placed a sufficient sum of money at my bankers which will be transmitted to Virginia as she needs it, and I do not anticipate any business difficulties arising to trouble you. In the event, however, of my death . . .'

'Ah! monsieur!' interrupted Mademoiselle Joseph, casting up her eyes and clasping her hands nervously together.

'In the event of my death,' continued Colonel Tennant, calmly, ignoring her exclamation, 'I should wish you to communicate with my lawyers. You will find their name and address within this envelope. Will you kindly place it in security, and communicate it to no one.   I have a special reason for this request.'

Mademoiselle Joseph drew out an antiquated pocket-book with silver clasps, and put the paper which he handed to her within it.

'It shall be safe with me,' she said, impressively.

'I have no doubt of it, my good Mademoiselle Joseph,' answered Colonel Tennant, smiling a little.   'I am trusting a far more precious possession to your keeping.'   He paused a moment, and then he said, gravely, ' I know very little of what may be the circumstances which will surround her, and I shall be powerless to control them. I want an assurance from you, Mademoiselle Joseph, that you will not leave her.   Let me feel satisfied that you will upon no pretext be prevailed upon to quit your post; whatever circumstance may arise, whatever others may think, let it be your duty to remain with Virginia.   It is possible that she may find, when I am gone, that she has no friend but you.'

'She may have many better friends,' cried the poor woman, wiping her eyes. 'But she will have none more faithful.'

'I believe it. You must tell her so from me when I am gone.'

He walked away to the table and came back again holding an open gold locket which enclosed a miniature of himself.

'You will give her this,' he said; and his voice shook a little. 'Give her this with my love when I am gone.'

'But you will see her again—in the morning,' cried Mademoiselle Joseph, aghast.

'See her again—perhaps,' he repeated, with a melancholy smile. 'But in the morning—no. I sail to-night. It is best. She will sleep now, and she will be spared the parting.'

'Ah, the poor child. My heart bleeds for her. What a waking!' and she burst into tears.

Colonel Tennant drew his brows together and a slight sternness gathered about his mouth. Mademoiselle Joseph's weaker sorrow jarred upon his own. He walked to the window and stood looking out into the night, but he only saw a girl's wet blue eyes and a sweet trembling mouth which he might never kiss again. The governess dared not break in upon his reflections. She remained silent, and furtively pressed her handkerchief to her eyes. She was too timid to take the initiative, and she made no movement to withdraw until the colonel, rousing himself from his abstraction, dismissed her.

'Good-night, Mademoiselle Joseph,' he said, 'good-bye. I know that you will do all in your power to guard Virginia. I trust you; you will not leave her till,' —he hesitated for an instant—' till I return. Adieu, my kind mademoiselle. Adieu.'

'*Au revoir*, monsieur,' she faltered, as

with hurried, uncertain footsteps she left
the room.

The sun was shining brightly over the
dazzling whiteness of the cliffs and the
blue waters of the Channel when Virginia
awoke. She opened her eyes and saw that
Mademoiselle Joseph, already fully dressed,
was seated at the foot of her bed. There
was something in the enforced calm of
her countenance, and in the compassionate
look she cast upon her, which struck terror
to the girl's heart. She raised herself upon
her pillows with wide questioning eyes,
and a gasping cry:

'Papa!'

'He sailed some hours ago, my poor
child,' cried Mademoiselle Joseph, trembling. 'He wished to spare you.'

But Virginia answered nothing. She
lay down again and turned her face to
the wall. No word or sigh escaped her.
For some minutes there was absolute

silence in the room. Then Mademoiselle Joseph approached, and, bending down, held out the locket.

'Your father left this beautiful likeness of himself for your consolation, my darling. See, is it not life-like?'

But Virginia did not move or turn to look at it, only her hand closed over the locket when it was laid beside her. She gave no other sign of consciousness.

'Ah, this is terrible,' sighed poor Mademoiselle Joseph, in her perplexity. 'I would rather that she had wept out her grief. This is worse than tears.'

But Virginia had not shed a tear; she lay still with her face turned from the light, and Mademoiselle Joseph did not venture to disturb her.

CHAPTER II.

For three days and nights after his departure Colonel Tennant's daughter kept silence. She went through the necessary routine of life as one who had lost all interest in it. She was not ungracious nor ill-tempered, but she answered Mademoiselle Joseph's anxious questions with gentle brevity, and for long hours she sat still and unoccupied or walked alone upon the sea-wall looking across the Channel.

On the fourth morning, however, she walked into the room with a step at once light and resolute and an air of having cast her troubles behind her.

'Dear mademoiselle!' she said, looking down at the thin nervous figure which was seated disconsolately at the table adding up accounts which invariably came wrong. 'You have been very patient. I will try you no longer. We will go to Stansfield to-day.'

'That is right. It is not that I wished to hurry you, my poor child, but if you can for your own sake put your sorrow aside . . .'

' I have foresworn its company,' Virginia interrupted her, a little quickly. 'And now let us pay our bills and get our affairs in order. There is a train in two hours' time by which we can reach Stansfield to-night.'

'But are they expecting us?'

'Certainly. My aunt wrote to say that she would be prepared to receive us any day after the 3rd, and this is the 6th.'

Mademoiselle Joseph raised no further objection, but in her own mind she was not altogether satisfied. It seemed to her that Virginia's entrance into the house of her unknown relations was a serious step in life, which should be undertaken with all due solemnity. It is true they were expecting her, and yet, as no day or hour had been decided upon, she would take them more or less unawares. Poor Mademoiselle Joseph felt very nervous. She busied herself about the preparations for their departure, but her mind was not at ease. She pasted wrong labels on the boxes, packed up the hotel blotting-book, and left her own purse in the drawer of the writing-table. It was Virginia who with deft quick fingers remedied her mistakes; it was Virginia who at last brought her bonnet and cloak and told her that the carriage was at the door. There was nothing more to be done. For an instant the girl paused upon the step, whilst her look passed over the line of the sea-wall to the expanse of waters now gleaming like a silver shield in the sunlight. As a frame encircles a picture so does the scene of our parting enshrine the memory of those we have lost. Several people had gathered in the hall to see the last of the girl about whom some of the visitors in the hotel had been pleased to weave an imaginary romance, but she did not notice them. Her eyes were full of tears as she stepped into the carriage.

'And so we start once more upon our travels,' cried Mademoiselle Joseph, with forced cheerfulness.

'Like Columbus in search of an unknown country,' replied Virginia, smiling.

It was late when they reached their last station. The country through which they passed, wood and valley, pasture and hill, had long been hidden from them by the misty darkness of an October afternoon; the scattered lights of the small country town alone warned them that they were approaching their destination, and they had still a drive of some miles before them.

Poor Mademoiselle Joseph sat in a forlorn and dejected attitude upon a bench whilst their luggage was being placed upon the sole fly which was in waiting. Virginia stood near her composed and patient. She had no doubt of her welcome, yet she was in no haste to receive it.

'Do you think that they will be prepared . . . that at this late hour your aunt will be glad of your arrival?' asked Mademoiselle Joseph, hesitatingly, as they were jolted in their unwieldy conveyance over the inequalities of the country lanes. She could but dimly see the girl's face by the uncertain lamplight as she turned towards her, but there was no shrinking or doubting in her answer.

'Certainly they will be glad to see us. You know it was my aunt's own wish that I should come to her. I am not afraid that they will not be glad.'

'No, of course, naturally not,' murmured the Frenchwoman; but nevertheless her heart beat with unaccustomed rapidity when, after passing through some lodge gates and up a wooded approach, the carriage stopped beneath a high portico, and the driver, descending, pulled with unnecessary violence at the bell. The clanging echoes were still sounding when the doors were thrown open, disclosing a large paved and well-lighted hall within. Mademoiselle Joseph was thankful to be able to remain behind under pretence of attending to the luggage, whilst Virginia followed the servant through a small vestibule into a long drawing-room beyond.

It had only one occupant, a girl, who in a loose white wrapper was half sitting, half reclining on a low couch near the fire. Her small feet were stretched out towards the blaze, from which the large fan that she held shaded her eyes. When Virginia was announced, and stood for an instant hesitating, though not shyly, upon the threshold, she half rose from her seat, and held out her hand, saying, in a tone of slightly aggrieved surprise :

'When she did not hear from you, mamma did not suppose that you would come to-day.'

Virginia came forward and stood upon the rug. She looked at Miss Stansfield with a grave astonishment. Brought up with but little practical experience of social observances, but under all the traditions of old-fashioned courtesy, it would have been instinctively impossible for her to be otherwise than polite to a guest, more especially to one who was, like herself, a stranger. She was not in the least embarrassed, not even discomfited, but she found it difficult to believe that this girl was her cousin, the only relation with whom she had as yet been brought into contact.

'I thought from what my aunt said in her letter that she was expecting me,' she said, calmly. She did not feel that any apology could be required from her. It was rather for Miss Stansfield to make what amends she could for the lack of welcome in her greeting. Virginia looked very slight and fair as she stood there in her dark travelling-dress, looking round with unabashed eyes, interested but not curious.

'Mamma is dressing. She will be down directly,' observed Miss Stansfield, indifferently; yet Virginia's composure had made a little impression upon her. She liked her the better for it. And then the door opened again; there was a scampering sound, and a dog's short bark in the passage, and, with a fat, long-haired terrier rolling like a ball of white worsted at her feet, a tall lady in evening-dress swept into the room.

'My dear child! So you have arrived!' she said, as she kissed her niece. 'Welcome to Stansfield.'

Her voice, though naturally metallic, was carefully modulated; it gave her a good deal of trouble, and so did the artistic arrangement of the elaborate plaits and waves of hair which were surmounted by a

slight apology for a widow's cap. Mrs.
Stansfield was a person who, upon principle,
made the best of everything which was in
any way connected with herself. 'I could
look ten years older to-morrow,' she said
to herself sometimes, 'but people need not
obtrude their age upon others. It is an
unpleasant fact and apt to become unsightly. I shall not be an old woman for twenty
years more. I shall keep age at a distance.'
And she derived a good deal of satisfaction from the sense of power. So far
she had succeeded, and she knew it. The
eyes with which she looked at Virginia were
as bright as her own; the hand which she
laid upon her shoulder was white and
slender.

'You must be tired and ready for
dinner,' she said; and all the while she was
scrutinizing her guest, noticing with impartial approval the pose of her head, the
grace of her light upright figure. 'Do not
wait to change your dress. Dinner will be

ready in ten minutes. My maid will un-
pack for you and show you your room. I
hope that your father left you well and in
good spirits?'

'Yes—thank you,' she answered, a little
quickly; then, looking round her: 'Have
you seen Mademoiselle Joseph?'

'I believe she has gone upstairs,' replied
Mrs. Stansfield, coldly. 'Emmeline, you
might go with Virginia.'

But Emmeline made no attempt to rise
from her chair; she began to cough,
and murmured something about being
afraid of the draughts. Virginia did not
wait for her mother to urge her. She
walked to the door and went out, closing
it behind her. In the hall she asked for
her room and Mademoiselle Joseph, and
ascended the stairs feeling a little puzzled
and a little indignant. In the corridor
above she paused in some uncertainty. It
was a large rambling country-house, in
which Stansfields had lived from time im-

memorial, adding to it from time to time as need arose. A passage ran all round the house above the square entrance hall, upon which doors opened leading into other parts of the building. Virginia had been told that her room was on the left in the west wing, but she fancied that she must have taken the wrong turning, and was about to retrace her steps when she was relieved to see a young man in evening-dress, evidently a guest of the house, advancing towards her.

'I have lost my way,' she said, standing still and looking at him with a frank inquiring smile.

'I shall be very happy if I may help you to find it,' he answered. Then, after an instant's pause, 'I think I must be right in supposing you to be my cousin— Virginia.'

He spoke her name gently, as if half afraid of being too familiar. But Virginia, so far from being offended, was very ready to respond to the first sincere word of welcome which she had received. Besides, this unknown cousin was hardly more than a boy. He was rather below middle height, with a pleasing deferential smile, brown hair parted in the middle, and a slight moustache.

'Yes, I am Virginia,' she answered, readily. 'And I see you must be Hartley. Now please tell me where I shall find my boxes and Mademoiselle Joseph.'

But at that instant Mademoiselle Joseph herself was seen emerging from a room some doors off, and Virginia hastened to her, only turning her head for a moment to say: 'I am afraid I must be late. Pray ask your mother not to wait for me.'

'Very well. I will keep a place for you by me,' he answered, quickly. But if it had been in his nature to be angry he would have been angered now by the scanty welcome she had received. One of them might at least have shown her to her room, he said to himself, as he went downstairs.

In the meantime, in the drawing-room below, Mrs. Stansfield was considering the position from her own point of view as she sat before the fire waiting for the re-appearance of her guest, with her silk skirts carefully arranged in their ample folds around her.

'The girl herself is presentable, indeed she is distinctly pretty, which is an un-doubted advantage; and, as to the ways and manners of society, if she is clever she may slip into them easily enough; but the companion!　Was there ever such an an-achronism!' cried the mistress of the house, with a gesture of surprised disgust. 'An antiquated demoiselle; provincialism incarnate which has unfortunately escaped all revolutionary aggressions.　One look at Mademoiselle Joseph is quite sufficient to dissipate any delusions as to elegance being inseparably connected with her nationality.'

'Has Virginia left the school-room?' asked Emmeline, languidly.

'My dear! Of course, she is nearly twenty.'

'Then we must find some means to keep the governess there,' answered Miss Stansfield. 'A governess without a school-room is most emphatically out of place.'

'You must be careful not to offend them,' said her mother. 'I never can understand why you should allow present comfort to take the place of every other consideration. You know that it is an object to me to have the girl here, and yet you will not raise a finger to help me. You are lazier than Hartley.'

'I am not fitted for active service, mamma. But at least I will promise you that mine shall be an armed neutrality.'

And Mademoiselle Joseph above was saying :

'Your excellent aunt was evidently a little unprepared for our arrival, but she is most amiable in her desire to disguise it. I trust, my darling, that you will be very happy here.'

'Yes, I shall like Stansfield,' answered Virginia. 'I am sure of it.'

She stood before the toilet-table fastening the coils of her hair round her charming head. She smiled at herself in the glass with a little air of resolution.

'I mean to be happy,' she was saying to herself. 'Why should I not be happy? It is good to have an aunt, it is delightful to have cousins. Since I cannot be with papa, or at La Vallière, I am glad to be here.'

'I am ready, mademoiselle!' she cried, gaily. 'Let us go down.'

CHAPTER III.

'THIS is a beautiful country,' said Virginia.
She had come in from a round of inspec-
tion. As soon as breakfast was over, she
had gone out alone into the gardens. She
had wandered under the reddening beeches
in the park; she had viewed with pleasure
the peaches in the high-walled kitchen garden. She had gathered a handful of autumnal
flowers, and greeted the old gardener with a
smile. It was a still fine day, and the light
mist of early autumn touched with sunlight lay like an aureole over the world.
As Virginia came into the drawing-room,
with her hat in one hand and her flowers
in the other, she had the kind of freshness

in her aspect which belongs to the morning
and to youth alone.

'What a pity that you should not be
able to be out of doors,' she said, looking
down at Emmeline, who with a book upon
her knees sat as usual close to the fire.
'The garden is delighful; you must be very
fond of Stansfield.'

Emmeline looked up, keeping her place
in the volume which she laid down reluctantly.

'Why should one be fond of a place?'

'Why!' echoed Virginia, opening her
eyes. 'How can one help it? As long as
this world is so beautiful, and one can spend
so many happy hours in it, I cannot understand how one can help it. When I think
of the rose garden at La Vallière, and the
old lime-tree at the gate . . . .'

She stopped suddenly and her eyes filled
with tears. Emmeline gazed at her, with
a growing curiosity which almost over-
powered her indifference.

'How very extraordinary and inconvenient,' she ejaculated. 'To be attached in this way to certain places is like a cat.'

'Is it?' asked Virginia, with unruffled good humour, swinging her hat lightly in her hand. 'But cats do not care for people, I believe.'

'Are you so unfortunate then as to care for people too?'

'I have not known many people,' answered Virginia. 'You know we lived almost alone at La Vallière. It was a solitary place, even the village was a mile away from us, and I had lived there ever since I can remember. I had only Mademoiselle Joseph and,' with an effort, 'papa to care for.' She paused a moment, as involuntarily with a sudden contraction at her heart her thoughts fled back to their parting, her last clinging embrace, and his unspoken farewell. And then she smiled and said, 'But there is no reason why I should not like other people as well.'

'I could find a great many reasons,' murmured Miss Stansfield.

'What are they?' asked Virginia, interested.

'They are hardly worth the trouble of recounting,' she answered, coldly. 'I have no doubt you will soon find them out for yourself.'

Virginia had seated herself on a low stool by the fire. She leaned her head upon her hand and looked thoughtful. Emmeline had taken up her book again, but after a few minutes, as she turned a page, she glanced at her companion.

'She is very pretty!' she said to herself, 'but I am dreadfully afraid she will bore me. I hate people who will ask inconvenient questions.'

'I must get some water for my flowers,' said Virginia, rising, 'and Mademoiselle Joseph wants me to help her in her arrangements; so *au revoir*;' and she left the room.

Emmeline drew her shoulders together

and raised her eyebrows. 'She actually seems to think that I shall miss her,' she murmured to herself. 'It is very absurd.'

That afternoon there was a sudden change in the weather. The sky became overcast, there were distant mutterings of thunder, and a low sighing wind swept the dead leaves along the ground. Mademoiselle Joseph, who had a constitutional dread of a storm, begged Virginia not to venture abroad, and the girl stood balancing herself on the step of the hall door, half amused at her fears and half inclined to rebel.

'But I like a storm,' she asserted. 'There is such spirit, such life in it. It carries everything before it, and sweeps away everything unsightly. I should like at this moment to be under those great beeches, as they bow their heads before it.'

'The most dangerous place you could select. When will you learn wisdom, my poor Virginia?   There are dangers enough in life without going to meet them.'

'I have not found this world at all a dangerous place,' answered the girl, smiling; 'still, it is true, I have not as yet seen very much of it.   Well! if I may not go into the gardens, I suppose I may safely explore the house.   There is a picture-gallery, and the library in the old wing, which I have not seen as yet.'

'I presume there could be no objection to your going over the house,' answered Mademoiselle Joseph, doubtfully.

'Why!' asked Virginia, surprised.   'It is not haunted, is it?   And, if it were, it would be a bold ghost indeed that would venture to walk in broad daylight.   Besides, if it is going to rain I shall want a book. I will go and explore this unknown country, and return to you with my spoils.'

She went back and crossed the tiled hall, stopping for a minute or two to examine the graceful carving and design of the

high mantel-piece. She passed the door
which led into the conservatory, and, pushing a heavy curtain aside, found herself in
the long passage which led down to the
rooms in the old wing of the house. No
modern improvements had changed its old-
fashioned aspect. To the back a mullioned
window looked out into the courtyard, a
well-worn stone staircase led to the floor
above, and a heavy oak door in the wain-
scoted passage, with deer's antlers above it,
was undoubtedly the library. As Virginia paused, Mrs. Stansfield's maid, Martin, a pleasant-mannered person, who had
already taken a fancy to her mistress's
young guest, came down the staircase on
her way to the housekeeper's room, with
some laces and ribbons in her hand.

'Is that the library?' asked Virginia,
pointing to the door before her.

' Yes, that is the library, miss,' answered
Martin, but without alacrity. 'Mr. Norton generally sits there.'

'Mr. Norton Stansfield,' repeated Virginia. Until now she had forgotten his existence. She had not seen him since her arrival, and, as it happened, no one had mentioned his name. She took a step forward and laid her hand upon the door. 'Since he is not here, I may certainly go in,' she said to herself. She turned the handle and entered.

She found herself in a long low room of irregular shape, lined with bookcases. In one of the many recesses there stood a draped easel, and in another a marble statue of Silence: a woman with her finger upon her lips. Some smouldering logs burned upon the wide hearth, and the light came shaded by overhanging creepers through the heavy stone frame-work of the window panes. The legitimate occupant of the room was seated at the table with a pile of papers and books before him. He was writing, with his brows slightly drawn together, and an air of absorbed application.

He did not raise his eyes at the soft opening of the door; but as Virginia closed it
behind her, and remained standing upon
the threshold, he looked up, and she met
his surprised gaze and coloured a little
under it, though she at once came forward
and said, with a frank smile:

'I did not know that anyone was here.
I hope that I have not disturbed you. I
came for a book. I thought that you were
away.'

'Why did you think that I was away?'

His manner, though not uncourteous,
was decidedly cold.

'Naturally I thought it when I never
saw you,' answered Virginia, somewhat
piqued. 'I came last night, I dined here,
I breakfasted here this morning. I have
just had luncheon with your mother and
your sister, yet you never appeared.'

'And you consider the dinner-bell to be
the roll-call of the family? Perhaps you
are right, but I do not always heed it.'

'Do you dine alone?'

'Sometimes,' he answered, briefly.

'How very dull!' observed Virginia. She had walked to the bookcase and was running her eyes along the titles of the books, which for the most part looked unpromising enough. 'Do you like to be alone?'

'Certainly, at times,' he answered, not without meaning.

'You mean that you wish me to go away?' There was not the least shade of offence in her voice as she took down a book and fluttered its pages. 'I see, you are busy. I will not stay long; but I must find a book.'

'I am afraid that you will not find anything there to interest you,' he answered, a good deal annoyed by the quickness with which she had divined a thought that he would on no account have put into words. 'There are some novels on the other side of the fireplace.'

'And I have hardly ever read any.' She promptly crossed the rug to the shelves which he had indicated. 'You know there are not many in French which young girls may read, and Mademoiselle Joseph is a severe critic. There are a great many books upon her index. Now this,' selecting a volume with a melodramatic frontispiece, and noting with pleasure the pages of dialogue. 'Now this looks excessively interesting.'

Mr. Stansfield glanced at the volume she held out, and, in spite of himself, he started.

'I think you had better not take that,' he said, quickly. He was angry at the position in which she had placed him. What was it to him? Why should he be forced, as it were, to give an opinion upon a subject with which he had not the slightest concern.

'I should like a love-story,' answered Virginia, laying down, however, the volume he had condemned and taking up another. 'Have you read this? shall I like it?'

He glanced at the author's name and assented shortly. He was anxious to free himself from the absurd pretension of acting as a guide to her inxperience. ' I cannot pretend to be a good judge of fiction,' he added; ' my food would probably be your poison.'

' Is that the reason that you will not dine with me?' asked Virginia, smiling again.

Mr. Stansfield felt as if a butterfly had flown in his face. This light onslaught upon the out-works of his natural reserve struck him as audacious, and yet it was so unconscious that it was not worth resenting.

' I hope to have the honour of dining with you some evening, Miss Tennant, though unfortunately to-night I have another engagement.'

' Miss Tennant!' echoed Virginia. ' Should

not cousins call each other by their Christian names ?'

'It is the custom; but it is my misfortune not my fault that I cannot claim any relationship with you.'

'Of course, I had forgotten for the moment that you are not Aunt Charlotte's son.'

'It was too heavy a price to pay even for the privilege of becoming your cousin,' muttered Norton, a slight smile just visible beneath his beard.

Virginia looked rather grave.

'I am sorry that you think so,' she remarked. 'She has been kind to me. But,' after a moment's reflection, 'I can hardly believe that she is papa's sister; she is not in the least like him.'

It was a question upon which he could not be expected to give an opinion, and she did not wait for an answer; but pausing for an instant before him with her book in her hand, she inclined her head slightly, wished him good-bye, and left the room.

'What did you find?' asked Mademoiselle Joseph. She looked up from her canvas work upon which various gorgeous floral specimens to be found in no botanical catalogue were strikingly pourtrayed. Virginia had returned to find her in the sitting-room to the west, which Mrs. Stansfield had carefully explained was to be for the special use of the governess and her charge. It was a pleasant little abode with pretty light chintz-covered furniture, and a window framed and festooned with crimson sprays of the virginian creeper which had twined itself round the stone balcony outside. 'What did you discover?' repeated Mademoiselle Joseph.

'I made no great discoveries,' the girl answered. 'I brought back this;' showing the volume she held; 'and I made the acquaintance of Mr. Norton Stansfield.'

'What is he like?' enquired Mademoiselle Joseph, with some veiled curiosity.

She bent her eyes once more upon her work, but she waited with her needle suspended for the answer.

'He has handsome dark eyes,' answered Virginia, slowly, 'and thick hair of a lighter colour with a wave in it, and a short beard . . . .'

'My dear child,' interrupted Mademoiselle Joseph, scandalized, 'I was not asking what you thought of Mr. Norton Stansfield's personal appearance.'

'Of what else could I have formed an opinion in a quarter-of-an-hour?' asked Virginia, in no wise disconcerted by the implied reproof. 'I do not know what more I can tell you. I feel sorry for him. He does not look very happy.'

'People are seldom very happy when their first youth is past,' observed Mademoiselle Joseph; she was apt to take refuge in generalities, when she was at a loss as to what to say about the special matter in question. 'The cares of life gather round them and cannot be dismissed at will. It is true, youth has its sorrows, but they are short-lived.'

'You are right,' cried Virginia. 'One cannot always be unhappy. The sun shines, and people are kind, and the world is beautiful, but still when one remembers . . .' She stopped short. 'I do not wish to remember,' she cried, passionately. 'I wish to be happy till he comes back; but he is always *here*,' pressing her hand upon her heart.

'My poor child, how you love him! You love him too much.'

'Can one help it?' asked Virginia, seating herself at the table, and resting her head upon her hands. 'I suppose that if people could kill what gives them so much pain they would do it; yet love is as strong as ever, is he not?'

'I really cannot say, my dear child. It is not a subject . . . in short, these speculations have, in my opinion, a morbid tendency.'

Virginia hardly heard her. She remained lost in thought. After a while she stepped out on the balcony. In the west, with stormy torchlights which seemed to flare in the wind to light him to his rest, the sun was sinking below the horizon. The grey heavens, flecked with light hurrying clouds, lay like a broken sea above, and Virginia, as she gazed, saw a white ship tossed upon it. She shivered and withdrew her eyes.

'I will be happy here,' she said to herself. 'They do not care for me as yet, but they will be kind to me. Perhaps after all kindness is better than love. It does not cost very much, and yet one can be grateful for it.' She went back into the room, and sat down by Mademoiselle Joseph.

'I do not think that Mr. Norton Stansfield is very fond of his step-mother,' she observed.

' That is very probable. It is a difficult position.'

' And why ?'

'The old Mr. Stansfield made a very peculiar will,' answered Mademoiselle Joseph, laying down her work and looking mysterious. ' Mr. Norton is his heir and yet he is not. This house is Mrs. Stansfield's for her life. If the eldest son is willing to remain here and manage the property, he has a right to do so ; otherwise, Mrs. Stansfield is at liberty to arrange matters as she pleases.'

' And if she were left to herself, she might injure the property? I understand ; but he would still inherit it.'

' Whatever was left of it,' replied Mademoiselle Joseph, shaking her grey curls. ' But only upon one condition.'

' What is that ?' asked Virginia, a little eagerly. She was growing interested.

'It is a very remarkable one. He is to remain at Stansfield as its master only if he is married at the time of his step-mother's death.'

'But why should old Mr. Stansfield have wished him to marry?' cried Virginia.

'Upon that point there are many different opinions. Some say the old man had a great wish for grandchildren. There had been, as it were, a curse upon the place, and for the last three generations the property had not gone in the direct line. Others say that, though he was a good deal under the dominion of his second wife, he always disliked and distrusted Hartley . . .'

'Stop; I will not hear any more,' cried Virginia, suddenly pressing her hands upon her ears. 'It is very shocking to think that you should have picked up all this gossip in so short a time, Mademoiselle Joseph. Who can have told you all these secrets.'

'They are no secrets to anyone.' The old Frenchwoman drew herself up with some dignity, and coloured with offence. ' I thought it my duty to learn all that was possible about those in whose family you were to be placed, and most of the facts were well known to me even before our arrival.'

'Then let us forget them, my good mademoiselle,' cried Virginia, gaily. ' I wish to be friends with everyone, so I must not hear anything against them, though, if I were to take a part, I know very well whose it would be.'

' Why, whose part should you take ?'

' Mr. Norton Stansfield's,' answered Virginia, decidedly.

' And why his more than another's ?'

' Because he is one and they are many. Besides, as I said before, he is not happy; I am sorry for him.'

' You need not be so,' cried Mademoiselle Joseph, sharply. ' It is not needful for you to be sorry for a man who has his happiness in his own hands, and besides is double your age.'

'But I am very sorry,' cried Virginia, laughing provokingly. 'It is unkind of you to espouse the opposite side. And Mr. Stansfield is not double my age. I should be still more sorry for him if he were.'

CHAPTER IV.

NEARLY thirty years before, a dark-eyed boy had hidden himself behind a curtain to watch with a dull weight of childish forebodings at his heart for the arrival of his father's new wife. Perhaps it was the fault of the old servants, who, ever since his mother's death, had combined to spoil the little Norton, and who now dreaded and disliked the advent of another mistress; but, when the boy thought of Mrs. Stansfield, his mind reverted to the big prints of Cinderella's step-mother frowning under a high feathered head-dress; and to the other cruel step-mothers of Grimm's fairy-tales.

Mrs. Stansfield, well-dressed and smiling, was very unlike anything his fancy had pictured, and yet, somehow, he did not like her any the better for it. He did not openly rebel against her authority—he was too proud to fight a losing game—and he very soon became aware that his father (his own natural protector) had gone over to the enemy's side; but he was of a sufficiently strong nature to hold aloof, and he did not care for her indulgence nor for the advantages which she had to offer. He received her amenities with unresponsive gravity, and, though at first Mrs. Stansfield had had some high notions of doing her duty towards the motherless boy, she very soon grew to feel him an unwelcome incumbrance; his silent disapproval embarrassed her, and she was jealous of her husband's affection for his first-born, which it was her constant endeavour to keep in check.

He was happy enough after his own fashion, as he grew older, with his gun and his fishing-rod. He knew every turn and pool in the river; every tree about the place. But it was an unnatural life for a child so young as he was at his mother's death. No one but the old housekeeper ever kissed him in his bed, no one asked about his lessons or showed interest in his play, and life had become already to him a serious thing when he was barely six years old.

Then there came a day when they told him that he had a little sister. Some one took him to see the infant laid among the white laces of its cradle, and asked him if she was not pretty. He shook his head gravely, yet some impulse made him stretch out a small, sun-burned hand, somewhat in need of soap and water, to touch the baby's softness; he long afterwards remembered his step-mother's querulous and hasty ex-postulation:

'Take care, nurse, pray do not let him touch the child.' Norton never attempted to do it again.

Then succeeded school-days, perhaps the happiest of his boyhood; and, naturally unsociable and reserved, he became studious. His masters said he was persevering rather than brilliant, and yet he had good abilities; perhaps he lacked spirit. He was a melancholy boy.

When Hartley came into the drawing-room before dinner and went prettily round to be kissed by all the ladies in turn, everyone said how very different he was from what his elder brother had been at the same age. He was never the least like Norton. When he grew older he could converse and take his place at the dinner-table with none of the shyness or constraint natural to a schoolboy, whereas Norton always took care to keep out of the way of strangers. Mrs. Stansfield said he was shy, but it was not so much shyness as a kind of instinctive pride which made him unwilling to go where he was uncertain of a welcome. Neglected and un-

noticed, he grew indifferent to other people.
He lived his life apart. Only a deep resentment smouldered within him when he
felt that, even to his father, he was of but
little account. He considered that he had
a right to his father's love, and felt himself
to be defrauded. He turned aside with a
demon of jealousy dragging at his heart
when Mr. Stansfield proudly showed off
his younger boy to strangers, or fondly
caressed his peevish little girl.

And when Norton left Oxford it was
not long before he discovered that his
position in his father's house was becoming untenable. A profession was spoken
of, but nothing was decided. Mr. Stansfield, as Norton bitterly thought, had no
care for his future; he was only anxious
to send him away. He should travel for
a year or two, so his father said, and see
something of the world. It would do him
no harm, even if he were to settle down
eventually to the life of an English squire.

And the year or two stretched itself out indefinitely. He travelled a good deal in the most unfrequented parts of Europe, then he started for America, and 'went West.' He was not unhappy, though he still made few acquaintances and no friends. He was at times as home-sick as a girl for the fields and woods of Stansfield. In his dreams he saw the sunlight on the quiet corn-fields, and heard the ripple of the river over the stones; but he never sought to return, he believed that no one wanted him.

It was a surprise to receive a sudden summons to his home. His father was ill, but he did not understand what that illness meant until he stood within the darkened room, and heard his voice.

'Is that you, Norton? Have you come back?'

'Yes, I have come back.'

He bent, and took the restless fingers upon the coverlet into his strong, firm

clasp. All recollection of individual wrongs
had long since passed away, yet, nevertheless, a sense of estrangement weighed upon
him, and made it difficult for him to speak.

'My eldest son!' the sick man repeated,
feebly. 'Never forget, Norton, that you
are my eldest son.'

He made no answer. What was there
to say? He thought, with some bitter-
ness, that it was his father who had hitherto been oblivious of the fact.

'You must undertake to carry out my
wishes, Norton,' Mr. Stansfield insisted,
half raising himself upon his pillows.
'Mrs. Stansfield does not understand; but
I—I am sorry if I have seemed to neglect
you.'

'Do not think of that,' said the young
man, quickly; the self-reproach hurt him,
it was not fitting from a father to a son.
'I have done very well. It was not your
fault.'

'But you promise. Dixon has all the

papers, and he understands my wishes. You will not fail me, Norton?'

'I will do all you wish, if it is in my power.'

Norton spoke distinctly yet softly, with instinctive comprehension of the needs of the poor flickering existence to which he had been called to minister in these last hours.

'The voice is Jacob's voice,' murmured the sick man.

'His mind wanders continually,' said some one who stood in the background. 'You had better leave him for the present.'

And he left him, never to hear another conscious word from his lips, never to receive any explanation of his last wishes except from the lawyer. But the lawyer was explicit enough, after his own cautious fashion. He trusted Norton Stansfield; he had known him from a boy. He had been often sullen, gloomy, and self-occupied, but he had never known him do a cruel action nor tell a lie. His father had believed in him too. It gave Norton a curious sense of satisfaction and regret to learn it now at the last; and his father's dying wish was that he might live upon the place, and that it might one day be his and his children's.

'It preyed upon his mind that Hartley would ruin himself and the estate, if it came into his hands,' so the lawyer said. 'If you care for his wishes, you will remain and do your best with it.' And so it was that he did remain the master of Stansfield; the unwilling guardian of his stepmother and her children.

They had nothing in common. Norton's education, though desultory, had not been superficial, he had read a good deal and had the keen insight of a spectator into life; yet there were many phases of it which he had never studied, simply because they had no interest for him; he had turned from them in indifference or disgust. Out

in the wilds of Colorado many strange
scenes had passed before him which had
left no more impression upon his mind
than the images of a dream; yet upon his
inward vision other little trivial pictures
were indelibly engraved: a tuft of ferns
by a mountain stream, the sunset reflected
in a solitary pool, the laughter in the eyes
of a little child. From these pure and
peaceful visions he stood equally apart, and
yet he felt that they held for him some
bond of union which he recognised in
silence. Between himself and the trifling
jealousies and petty ambitions of a disappointed woman there was no such tie of
fellowship. He was determined to carry
out his father's dying wish, but he sometimes
felt that he had a heavy price to pay for
his loyalty to the dead. It is an allegiance
which cannot be broken, a service from
which there is no enfranchisement.

It was three years since his father died,
and he saw no prospect of release from a

duty which became every week more irksome; and yet there was a fund of obstinacy in his nature which made him unwilling to own himself worsted. He avoided as much as possible any personal encounters with his stepmother; he ignored her wishes when he felt it impossible to carry them into effect, but when there were no important issues at stake he was quite ready to let her take her own way. She often imagined that she had circumvented him by stratagem, when in reality he had looked on at her tactics with contempt or indifference.

On one occasion Hartley, with his habitual ease of manner shaken into something like fear, had of his own accord sought his brother's help. He had something to say, and Norton would give him no assistance. ' He had been unfortunate, he saw now he had been a fool, but what was to be done, the money must be paid.' Norton made no observation, he did not seem surprised;

perhaps he knew more than had been told in that halting confession in which a little genuine shame was hidden beneath boyish effrontery. He heard him in gloomy silence, and then he wrote a cheque and handed it to him. ' It will be for the last time,' that was all that he said; and he never in any way by look or word referred to it again. He had no wish to receive confidences from his step-mother, or to give them. She believed in Hartley, he had no desire to undeceive her. There was only one thing which he absolutely required at Mrs. Stansfield's hands, and that was the undisturbed possession of his own rooms. He dined when he pleased alone and at his own hours, and it was very rarely that any member of the family even knocked at the library door.

It was an unwelcome surprise when a few weeks after Virginia's arrival Mrs. Stansfield sought him there. She entered into many apologies, but he perceived to his discomfiture that she had seated herself in his most comfortable arm-chair and seemed to be prepared for a protracted interview.

'Norton,' she began, after a somewhat ominous pause, 'I have come to have a little private talk with you. I have come to consult with you.'

Norton knew perfectly well the meaning of that preface in general. It meant that his step-mother intended to take her own way. He waited to let her open the campaign; distant but courteous.

'A great responsibility rests upon me,' continued Mrs. Stansfield. 'I almost fear that it is one which I should not have undertaken. Yet how could I refuse my brother's most natural request that I would take care of Virginia in his absence?'

'I am sorry if you feel it to be a burden. I am afraid,' said her step-son, with a slight smile, 'that it is one from which I cannot relieve you. Yet why should you feel it a burden?　Miss Tennant already has made up her mind to find Stansfield charming.　She is not therefore very difficult to please, and she appears to me to be well able to take care of herself.'

'It is not a question of her amusement.' Mrs. Stansfield spoke with some asperity. 'I should be hardly likely to consult you about that.'

'You are right.　I should not know how to amuse Miss Tennant; yet how am I qualified to give any other advice about her?'

'She is at such a difficult age,' sighed Mrs. Stansfield, 'neither woman nor child.'

'It is a delightful age,' answered Mr. Stansfield, 'when the present is but the antechamber to the future.　But, indeed, I think she told me, with much unnecessary pride, that she is twenty.'

'That proves what I have just said— she is a perfect child.　What girl with any knowledge of the world would wish, even in her first youth, to make her age known to everyone?'

'That is true. She might easily have passed herself off for eighteen.'

He smiled rather grimly.

'She might,' answered Mrs. Stansfield, unobservant of the sarcasm. 'And, as I said before, I wish that she were either younger or older. She is too young to have any prior attachment, and yet old enough to be in love.'

'If that is a danger to be averted, I should say that she has done well to come to Stansfield,' observed Mr. Stansfield, seriously.

'I wish I could think so, but I cannot be so oblivious as you are of your brother's existence.'

'Hartley!' he exclaimed, with a slight gesture of contempt. 'I confess I had forgotten Hartley.'

'Hartley is, however, two years older

than Virginia. He already admires her, and I confess that I have my misgivings. If her father were at home and at hand to take the responsibility and ready to give his consent, it would be another matter; but, as it is, I am placed in a very awkward position. Virginia is under my care; she is an only daughter and an heiress. What would be said if I permitted her to entangle herself with my son? Would it be right,' continued Mrs. Stansfield, slowly fixing her eyes upon Norton, 'would it be honourable to allow her to form an attachment with *anyone* until she has had an opportunity to see something of the world? Might she not easily, at her age, fall a victim to her inexperience?'

'I have no great faith in the wisdom of maturity,' answered Mr. Stansfield. 'But really, upon a personal question like this, I have no opinion to offer.'

'Yet you may help me. Young men

understand each other. You might observe
and tell me if you see any danger of
Hartley's . . .'

'Stay,' cried Norton, interrupting her,
'I could do nothing of the sort. I have
no desire to interfere with Hartley's freedom of action, no right to constitute myself
guardian to Miss Tennant.'

'Then you refuse to help me?'

He got up, looking provoked, and walked
to the window.

'In this matter certainly.'

'I wish you were not so unsympathetic,'
murmured his step-mother. 'I get very
little encouragement to confide in you.'

But when she soon afterwards left the
room she knew well enough that she had
accomplished all that she desired. Her words
might readily at some future time recur to
his mind: 'Would it be right or honourable to let her entangle herself with *anyone*
in her father's absence before she had seen
something of the world?' Norton was, as

she had said, unsympathetic; he had a bad moody temper; she could never understand him; but he had absurdly high-flown ideas of honour. After what she had said, he, at least, would not take advantage of Virginia's inexperience.

CHAPTER V.

'But I only promised to maintain an armed neutrality,' said Miss Stansfield. 'I already find my arms rather heavy. I am quite incapable of using them.

She was reclining upon the sofa with a shawl round her shoulders, and her head laid back upon the cushions. Her mother sat bolt upright on a chair at a little distance, and wore her most business-like aspect.

'This is a childish evasion, Emmeline. I am not talking of fighting. You know that I should be the last person to desire strife; I only ask you not to drive the girl away.'

'I have no wish to drive her away. I thought at first that she would be wearisome, but, on the contrary, she rather amuses me. There is something original in her determination to be happy, and to make friends with everyone. It is quite funny to see the way in which she receives your amenities, for instance.'

'Then why cannot you exert yourself to be civil to her?'

'Because, my dear mother, that would be to reverse altogether our proper positions. It is her business to amuse me.'

'I am afraid that, if she is left so much alone, she will begin to dislike Stansfield,' said Mrs. Stansfield, fussily. 'And it is so important that she should remain.'

'And yet you say you are afraid of dissensions? You wish Hartley to fall in love with her. Have you never thought that Norton may do so also?'

'It would do him no harm, and it would do Hartley a great deal of good. There is nothing like marriage to steady a young man.'

'Especially when the young lady is an heiress!' observed Emmeline, with a touch of sarcasm. 'Still, mamma, you have not answered my question, what is to be done if she attracts them both. It strikes me that the situation would be awkward.'

'A girl of that age would never think of Norton,' answered Mrs. Stansfield. 'And, as I said before, he is well able to take care of himself. Now it is imperatively necessary that Hartley, on the contrary, should fall in love with her.'

'Oh dear, oh dear! a love-affair in the house is so fatiguing!' sighed Miss Stansfield, raising her head for a moment to arrange herself more comfortably upon the pillows. 'Surely you do not expect me to have anything to do with it.'

'I expect you to show a little sisterly sympathy.'

'If it is to be shown in making love for

my younger brother, I am sure I shall
never succeed. It would be almost as bad
as making love for oneself. Besides, I
could never plead Hartley's cause. He
would not make a good husband.'

'Why not?' asked her mother, with a not
unnatural flush of anger.

'He is so selfish!' and Emmeline half
closed her eyes as if the light hurt them.
'I hate Norton, but, after all, he is worth
ten of him.'

To this Mrs. Stansfield, affronted, made
no answer. She got up, and walked away
to the fire-place, and began to push the
poker noisily about among the coals.

'And I have a head-ache already,' murmured Miss Stansfield from among her
cushions; but her complaint passed un-
heard or unheeded.

She lay still, as if asleep, but all the
while she watched her mother from under
her drooped eyelids.

'Emmeline, be reasonable for once,' said

Mrs. Stansfield at last, coming back and seating herself upon the end of the sofa. 'You at least agree with me in one thing: you wish Norton to leave the house?'

'Yes, I do wish it;' speaking with more animation than she had hitherto displayed. 'There is always something to make one uncomfortable when he is in the background. It is like thunder in the air. And he will have his own way. He would not have the beech-tree cut down which keeps the sun from my bed-room window. He has no consideration. I am sure I should be more comfortable if he were gone.'

'And you think he is likely to fall in love with Virginia?'

'How can I tell? She is very pretty, and men are such fools,' answered Emmeline, in her gentle invalid's voice.

'Then do you not see that we have the game in our own hands?' cried Mrs. Stansfield, excitedly. 'If he cares for Virginia, and she marries Hartley, will he be likely to remain in the house with her? He has fought a hard battle to maintain his position here, but he will be driven from it at last.'

'If battles were always won by strategy, there would be no doubt of your success, mamma. I wonder that you can carry it all in your head; it is so bewildering.'

'Not at all. It is as simple and plain as possible; and justice would be done at last.'

Mrs. Stansfield walked across the room and came back again. Her face was a little flushed; some angry passions had left their traces upon it. She looked ten years older than when she was dressed for the evening, and went with smiling dignity to take her place at the head of the table.

'It is like an arithmetical problem,' observed Miss Stansfield, with a smile as cold as wintry sunlight. 'If Norton and Hartley love Virginia, and Virginia loves

Hartley . . . but what if she should love Norton?'

'I tell you it is impossible,' said Mrs. Stansfield, angrily.

'Well, I only hope they will not trouble me about it.' She drew her shawl more closely round her, and in a few minutes was wrapped in a genuine slumber. 'I hope my head will not ache when I wake up,' was her last conscious thought.

When, an hour later, she awoke, to find that her mother had left the room, and that Mr. Stansfield had just entered it, she looked up at him, and said,

'It is better now.'

'What is better?' he asked, perplexed.

'My head-ache. It was very bad this morning. I was afraid it would not go away all day; but I have been asleep, and it is decidedly better. What o'clock is it?'

'Nearly four.'

He did not take the trouble to congratulate her.   Possibly Emmeline's head-aches were well-worn subjects of conversation.

'Still six hours before bed-time,' sighed Miss Stansfield. 'And how cold and miserable it looks out of doors;' raising herself on the sofa, and turning her eyes listlessly towards the window. 'Yet, I declare, there is some one crossing the lawn. Do see who it can be. I am not equal to visitors; or is it only Virginia?'

Mr. Stansfield looked in the direction indicated as desired, but without manifesting any interest.

'Yes, it is Miss Tennant,' he answered.

'I wonder what some people are made of!' ejaculated Miss Stansfield; she was so far moved as to walk to the window. Virginia was coming across the grass towards the house in her dark, close-fitting morning-dress, with her head uncovered, trailing something along the ground, and playing with an ungainly Newfoundland puppy which gambolled at her heels.   She had a basket in her left hand, and as she came nearer she smiled and nodded her head at the window, and held it up in triumph.

'Can you guess what is in it?' she cried, in her high, young voice. 'Wait a moment and you shall see.'

She ran round to the hall door, and a few minutes later entered the drawing-room. Some raindrops shone on her bright hair; the wind had brought the colour to her cheeks; her skirts were heavy with moisture.

'Where have you been? You will most certainly catch cold, Virginia, and I cannot bear anyone else to be ill in the house,' was Miss Stansfield's querulous greeting.

'Why should I be ill? I am never ill,' answered the girl, laughing softly. 'I have been into the copse by the river, and the brambles were rather wet, but I have robbed them to some purpose. Look here!' and she showed her basket full of ripe blackberries.

'Oh! dear, I hope you are not going to eat all those, or you will be ill, if you have never been ill before.'

'They are delicious,' answered Virginia, selecting one of the biggest and putting it into her mouth, 'and I never heard of anyone but the babes in the wood who were the worse for them. Will you have some?' holding out her basket to Mr. Stansfield with a smile.

'I am afraid I am hardly worthy.' But his gravity relaxed a little as he put his fingers into the basket.

'You must leave some for Mademoiselle Joseph,' said Virginia, seriously. 'And where is Aunt Charlotte?'

'Yes, where?' he echoed, addressing himself to Emmeline. 'I came here to find her.'

'I believe that she is in the book-room.'

'With Marshall?' asked Mr. Stansfield, with an emphasis on the word.

'How should I know?' asked Emmeline, fretfully. But he was silent and looked pre-occupied.

'Who is Marshall?' asked Virginia.

'What questions you ask,' said her cousin. 'You surely must have seen Marshall. He is mamma's prime adviser. I should call him our steward; but I do not know by what title he describes himself.'

'By an honourable one, no doubt,' observed Mr. Stansfield, sarcastically. 'I am afraid I cannot wait until his deliberations with your mother are over. But please tell her that I dine at home to-night.'

'I must go to Mademoiselle Joseph,' said Virginia, taking up her basket.

'Why should people have enemies?' she said to herself as she mounted the stairs.

'Yet I am sure that his step-mother is Mr. Stansfield's enemy. Why should she dislike him? He has handsome eyes and a pleasant voice. I like him. I am sorry that he is unhappy. Perhaps he has been in love and has been deceived. Yet I should not think it. Perhaps Aunt Charlotte wants to drive him away, so that Hartley may have the property. But I do not believe that she will be able to do it, and I am very glad of it,' thought Virginia.

She paused for a minute in the embrasure of a passage window to watch the last red glimmer of the sinking sun. Down in the corridor below a door stood ajar, and she heard her aunt's voice saying,

'It must be done at once, and you must promise him whatever compensation he asks.'

'I will do my best, Mrs. Stansfield,' answered a man's voice, 'but you must remember that Mr. Norton may choose to inquire . . .'

Virginia passed on and heard no more.

'I would rather trust Mr. Stansfield than Aunt Charlotte,' she thought to herself. 'I suppose that is Marshall talking with her, and he must be on her side.'

In the little sitting-room the fire burned brightly and the lamp was already lighted. Mademoiselle Joseph sat in the arm-chair with a volume of Racine in her hands. It was nothing to her that her presence in the house was, as far as it was possible, ignored by all except Virginia. Her placid existence made no demands upon the interest or consideration of others. If she regretted her own country, and the trivial but to her important concerns of her native village; if she felt herself a stranger uninvited and disregarded, she made no complaint. Her aim was simple enough; it was to be a faithful friend and guardian to

Virginia Tennant until her father's return. As a dog watches at his master's command with absolute and unreasoning fidelity, so she would watch over the young girl who had been committed to her care. For herself she asked and expected nothing. It was natural that she should love Virginia. She had nothing else to love. Any evidence of the girl's fondness for her gave her constantly recurring and pleasurable surprise. She often trembled for the child, and felt powerless to protect her. For youth, to her, was a season of peril; like the springtime of the year, it is subject to sudden alternations, devastating storms, and cruel frosts. The sunshine betrays, and there is a false promise in its chill brightness. Through this season Virginia, alas! must pass with a spirit which knew no fear, with a high hope which should most surely be dashed to the ground. Well! some day Virginia would acknowledge that she was right, and poor Mademoiselle Joseph sighed and took refuge in her cross-stitch and her Racine.

Virginia had seated herself on a low stool by the hearth. Her hands were clasped round her knees, her eyes were bent upon the glowing fire which had brought a slight flush to her cheeks.

'Had you ever an enemy, Mademoiselle Joseph?' she asked suddenly, after some minutes of thoughtful silence.

'Indeed, I should hope not,' answered the old Frenchwoman, closing her book and putting it back carefully upon the table. 'I trust that I have given no one any occasion to desire to injure me.'

'And I have never had an enemy, either, Mademoiselle Joseph. It strikes me that we are two very fortunate people.'

But Mademoiselle Joseph would not be betrayed into congratulation.

'One never knows what may happen.

It is not likely that anyone would take the trouble to hate me; but as for you, Virginia . . .' and she shook her head mournfully.

'And why then should they hate me?' cried Virginia.

'Because of your many good gifts, my poor child. Young and prosperous, pretty and rich.'

'Rich!' echoed the girl, 'I never knew that I was rich.'

'I thought . . . I supposed. It is not a fact upon which it is advisable to dwell,' cried Mademoiselle Joseph, confused by her own indiscretion.

'I cannot see why not. I am very glad of it. Yes, I am glad that I am rich. To be rich is to be at ease, and to have the power of making other people happy; to be rich is to be free from sordid anxieties; to be rich . . .'

'To be rich,' interrupted Mademoiselle Joseph, 'is to be the subject of envy and perhaps dislike to those who are less fortunate than yourself.'

' My riches are not so apparent as to raise any bad feelings in others. They were not even manifest to myself.'

' Yet you knew surely that your father never denied you anything ?'

' Love is always prodigal of gifts,' answered the girl, quickly. ' They were evidences of affection not of wealth.'

Mademoiselle Joseph shook her head and smiled a little indulgently as if amused at the girl's simplicity.

' Well! you cannot make me think otherwise,' cried Virginia. ' To be poor is to have little to give and little to enjoy —I am very glad that I am not poor. I am very glad that I am rich.'

She stood up and shook back the hair from her forehead.

' And now, mademoiselle!' she said, a little imperatively, ' I will take my work if you will read to me.'

CHAPTER VI.

FOR the first time since Virginia's arrival there was to be a dinner-party at Stansfield. It was the manner in which Mrs. Stansfield generally chose to entertain her friends. She had the eye of a general for the disposal of her guests, and at a less informal gathering it annoyed her to feel that they were apt to escape from her control. In spite of her most strenuous efforts young men sought out the wrong young ladies; those whom she wished to keep apart found subjects in common; those whom she desired to distinguish remained unnoticed; and others whom she would have suppressed were encouraged and admired.   At a dinner, on the other hand, she was for the greater part of the evening mistress of the situation ; whatever people might feel they were bound to disguise their sentiments, and in the consciousness of good wine and a well-cooked dinner Mrs. Stansfield felt that she was well able to compensate them for any personal disappointments.   No one with a well-chosen *menu* before them had a right to complain.

On the afternoon of this particular day, however, she had received a slight shock to the assured complacency with which she generally looked forward to a well-arranged party.   Norton, upon whom she had reckoned to take his proper place as master of the house, had declined to be present.   He had no real or sufficient reason for absenting himself, but he had business which would detain him in the neighbouring town, and he had arranged to dine there rather than at home.   Even in such a trivial matter as this she knew that it would be in vain for her to attempt to alter his determination; but she felt herself to be justly annoyed. His absence might occasion unfriendly comments and make known to others the absence of harmony among the members of her household. Mrs. Stansfield was above all things desirous of showing a good front to the world and by no means wished to make public any family dissensions. Norton, to do him justice, was as reticent as she could desire, but on this occasion she felt that he was treating her unfairly. Mrs. Stansfield was, it is true, of a self-sufficient nature; but still it was dispiriting to make festive preparations unaided and alone. Hartley was returning home that evening only in time for dinner, and Emmeline was dividing her attention between a headache and a new book. As Mrs. Stansfield sat at her writing-table somewhat gloomily writing her guests' names on slips of paper,

Virginia, fresh and smiling, broke in upon her solitude.

'The table looks very well indeed, Aunt Charlotte. That scarlet begonia in the centre has an excellent effect. When it is lighted, it will be beautiful,' cried Virginia, looking delighted.

Mrs. Stansfield looked up at the girl and could not help smiling kindly in answer. 'What a ridiculous child she is,' she said to herself; nevertheless, this spontaneous touch of sympathy called for some response. It was as if a warm hand had suddenly closed round her chilled fingers.

'I am glad that it looks so well,' she said, relapsing into her ordinary manner. 'Martin has great taste in arranging flowers. This will be your first English dinner-party, I suppose.'

'It will be my first anywhere,' answered Virginia. 'I have never (would you believe it!) I have never been to any parties or receptions. Papa did not care for them.

I am very glad that you have some friends invited for this evening. I have been thinking of it all day,' cried the girl, laughing a little softly.

'I hope you may not be disappointed.' Mrs. Stansfield's tone was sufficient to have chilled any anticipations of pleasure as she bent again over her papers. But Virginia did not heed it. She went away singing through the passages after having cast another glance of approval upon the dining-room table.

'I shall wear my white silk and my pearls,' she said, as she stood before her pier-glass that evening. Her morning dress lay upon the ground at her feet, her white rounded arms and shoulders were uncovered, her brown hair partly unloosened fell in soft waves about her throat. Mademoiselle Joseph, glancing up at her, thought that no adornment could make her prettier than she was at that moment ; but aloud she only said,

'If it is not a large party, may not the dress or at least the pearls be out of place? I have heard that it is the fashion here for young girls to dress with great simplicity.'

'Nevertheless, I shall wear my silk dress and my pearls, mademoiselle. What is the use of having pretty things if they are to be hidden away; and I love my pearls. Papa gave them to me.' She drew them out of the case and slipped the string lightly through her fingers. 'I wish to look my best to-night.'

'Why to-night?'

'Why, because there will be so many guests, of course.'

'It is perhaps a less dangerous reason than that which may prompt the same wish on other occasions,' answered Mademoiselle Joseph, solemnly.

'You are always thinking of dangers,' cried Virginia, a little impatiently. 'What dangerous reason could I have for wishing to look my best?'

'The wish to please one rather than many.' And Mademoiselle Joseph sighed. 'It is then that remonstrances cease to be of any avail, and pride itself is no safeguard.'

Virginia looked puzzled.

'I think that if I wished to please one person only I should choose Mr. Norton Stansfield,' she said, calmly.

Poor Mademoiselle Joseph let her knitting fall upon her knees, the stitches slipped unheeded from the needles, whilst with uplifted hands she ejaculated,

'*De grâce*, Virginia, do not say such terrible things.'

'I see nothing terrible in it, dear mademoiselle.' Virginia had returned to the dressing-table and was fastening the pearls in her small ears. 'But it would be a difficult task. I feel sure that Mr. Stansfield would not be easily pleased.'

'Then pray do not attempt it,' pleaded Mademoiselle Joseph, earnestly. 'He who approaches the fire will be burnt.'

'Say rather he who touches an iceberg will be frozen,' cried the girl, lightly. 'I do not think that you need be afraid of Mr. Stansfield. You would not even allow me to be sorry for him. I was sorry. I do not think that he cared about it.'

'He is evidently of a morose disposition. He is unsociable and the reverse of domestic. No one in the house has anything in common with him. We need not trouble ourselves about Mr. Norton Stansfield, Virginia.'

'Still for all that I like him, Mademoiselle Joseph.'

'How self-willed is youth,' murmured the poor governess, discomfited; but she judged it prudent to change the conversation.

The drawing-room was already full of guests when Virginia came in. She made her entrance under the shelter of some other arrivals, and for a moment or two remained unnoticed. Hartley alone, who

was never deficient in small attentions,
came up to present a bunch of autumn
violets.

'Is it permitted to compliment you upon
your dress?' he asked.

'Certainly; I am glad that you like it.
Papa bought it for me when we were in
Paris.' Then, in a lower tone, 'Has every-
one arrived?'

But he was not allowed time to answer
the question. Mrs. Stansfield caught sight
of her niece, and rustled forward to make
some formal introductions. Her manner
was at once patronizing and apologetic,
proud and deferential. She was well
aware that Virginia had many social deficiencies, for which she wished to beg
forbearance, yet she was in a measure
proud of her natural advantages, and
desired that they should be acknowledged.
But not even this ordeal had any power
to disturb Virginia's self-possession. She
saw a good many well-dressed people in a

well-lighted room and she was interested, but she was by no means dazzled. Of too frank a nature to be critical, she was ready to accept their expressions of kindness for perhaps more than they were worth; she did not claim anything from them as a right, still less would she be likely to take anything from them as a favour. She did not feel that she was dependent upon their opinion, and she was not concerned about it; but she was ready to be amused.

Emmeline, who looked paler than usual, in a light-pink gown and with white flowers in her hair, glanced up at her with a sort of fretful astonishment, and Virginia bent her head to ask,

'What is the matter? You look tired already. Does your head ache?'

'Not more than usual. It is not wonderful that I should look tired. It is much more wonderful that you should look happy.'

'It is not so difficult,' answered the girl, smiling.

'Is it not? It is an art which I have never acquired.'

'An art!' echoed Virginia, perplexed.

'What an absurdity it is not to be able to understand what one means,' cried Emmeline.

'What is it that she does not understand?' asked Hartley, coming up. 'Will you allow me to enlighten your ignorance, Virginia? That little Captain Damer is to take you in to dinner; but I shall be on your other side.'

'Where is your brother?' she asked, looking round.

'Are you ambitious of sitting next the master of the house? Well,' with a rather unpleasant laugh, 'you will not have that honour this evening. He is not at home.'

Virginia made no answer. She drew up her small head with an air of displeasure, and for the first time he felt that he had presumed upon his relationship. It was true he had annoyed her, and she did not hesitate to show it. Yet when he murmured an apology she met it with her usual frankness.

‘I was only sorry that he should miss the party,’ she said, simply ; and then Mrs. Stansfield brought up Captain Damer to be introduced, and they all went in to dinner.

‘Is not the table pretty ?’ asked Virginia, in a low voice, smiling at her cousin. Then her eyes travelled past the scarlet begonia and over the heads of the guests. Yes, she had seen them all, not one had escaped her notice, and her fair cheeks flushed, and an indignant light came into her eyes.

‘Hartley,’ she said, once more turning her head towards him. ‘Where is Mademoiselle Joseph ?’ And, as he did not answer for a moment : ‘Why,’ in a clear, indignant voice, ' why is not Mademoiselle Joseph here?'

' I am not sure. I believe she did not wish to come down. Do not distress yourself about it.' But he in his turn had changed colour.

' I understand,' she answered. ' She was not considered to be fit to meet your friends. Then I am not fit either.'

' My dear cousin,' he said, deprecatingly, ' Captain Damer is speaking to you.'

But his remonstrance and Captain Damer's half-formed sentence alike passed unheeded.

' I am sorry to seem uncourteous,' she said, calmly, as she rose from the table, ' but I must go to her.'

In another moment she had pushed back her chair and slipped out of the room. There was a hush in the conversation, whilst Mrs. Stansfield's inquiry, ' What is it? Is Virginia ill?' was followed by a buzz of interrogations.

'She was overcome for the moment,' answered Hartley, smoothly. 'The heat of the room,—the flowers are somewhat strong. She begged that no one would disturb themselves for her.'

But Mrs. Stansfield had already formed a correct surmise as to the cause of Virginia's disappearance. She knew that an untruth came easily to Hartley. It was to him a well-proved weapon. Mrs. Stansfield felt that he was right. Virginia had treated her badly, but it was most prudent to disguise it. Nothing was in such bad taste as a family quarrel. So she went on calmly with her dinner, merely giving orders that her maid should be sent to attend upon Miss Tennant.

But the maid sought her in vain. Virginia had left the dining-room upon the impulse of the moment, but she was in no mood to regret what she had done. At the same time as she paused in the empty hall she felt herself to be in a difficulty.

She had said she would go to Mademoiselle
Joseph, but she now remembered that to
do so would only be a fresh source of
trouble to one whom she desired to defend.
It would be easy for Mademoiselle Joseph's
placid spirit to accept neglect and isola-
tion as her natural lot; it would be a tor-
ment to her to believe that Virginia, upon
her account, was about to embroil herself
with her relations.

Virginia thought of it all as she stood
doubting, hesitating, under the light of
the hall-lamp. The housemaids were
already busied in putting the drawing-
rooms in order, and she could not take
refuge there. Her bed-room was as yet
fireless. Suddenly a thought struck her—
she might have the library and its fire to
herself; and, if she were obliged to miss
her dinner-party, she would at least con-
sole herself with a novel. She crossed the
hall, turned down the dimly-lighted passage, and opened the library door. She

was not disappointed : a bright fire burned upon the hearth, a lamp stood lighted upon the table. She sat down in a low chair and spread out her hands to the flame.

She was not long left in solitude. After ten minutes or so, there were steps in the corridor, the door was unhesitatingly opened, and her retreat was invaded. But Virginia would not look up. No doubt her aunt had sent some one in search of her ; but indignation still held the mastery, and she would not be appeased. She leaned her bare rounded arms upon her knees, rested her head upon her hands, and still remained staring resolutely at the fire.

'Are you aware that they have gone in to dinner, Miss Tennant?' asked a man's voice.

Mr. Stansfield had closed the door behind him, and advanced a few steps into the room. He was in morning dress, and held some papers in his hand. He was looking down at Virginia with an air of grave inquiry, not unmixed with dissatisfaction. It was evident that her presence did not strike him in the light of an agreeable surprise. His voice recalled Virginia to herself.

She looked up, and said, with a somewhat rueful smile,

'I know that they are at dinner; but I came away.'

'Were you not well?'

'Oh, yes, I was perfectly well, and—very hungry.'

'Then what drove you away? Was it too tiresome? Were you bored?'

'On the contrary, I was expecting to enjoy myself. I had been looking forward to it all day.'

'To have had a whole day's pleasure out of a party is surely as much as you could expect,' observed Mr. Stansfield, setting down his candle. 'It would have been unreasonable to have demanded an evening's enjoyment as well.'

'But I did expect it,' she answered.

She leaned her brown head back against the cushions of her chair, and looked rather grave.

'Then what drove you into solitary confinement?'

'I thought it was unkind not to have asked Mademoiselle Joseph;' and tears of hurt feeling gathered in her blue eyes. 'It was a kindness which would not have cost them very much. I could not sit at a table where she, my best friend, was not welcome.'

A serious smile, which had no mockery in it, touched Mr. Stansfield's lips.

'Have you forgotten that the days of chivalry are past? You will surely not be so unwise as to fight in anyone's quarrels but your own?'

'Well, I could not help it this evening.'

Then, with a smile and a sigh: 'It has cost me my dinner.'

'That misfortune can at least be remedied.'

'No,' cried Virginia, 'I cannot, I cannot go back to the dining-room.'

'And yet you are very hungry?'

'Very,' answered Virginia, with emphatic sincerity.

'And, no doubt, there were a great many excellent dishes. Mrs. Stansfield is famous for her dinners.'

'There was ice cream and meringues,' answered Virginia, sighing a little.

'Ice cream and meringues,' repeated Mr. Stansfield, thoughtfully. 'Do you know, I am not quite sure that the occasion demands so great a sacrifice.'

'It does. I shall not go back to the dining-room, Mr. Stansfield.'

'Then, if Mahomet will not go to the mountain, the mountain must come to Mahomet.'

He rang the bell, and ordered the servant who answered it to bring in some supper.

'I believe,' he said to the sedate but surprised footman, 'I believe there is an ice cream and some meringues.'

'How kind you are!' cried Virginia, delighted. 'I hope that Mrs. Stansfield will not be angry.'

But Mr. Stansfield's smile said plainly that Mrs. Stansfield's anger was a matter of supreme indifference to him.

The little round table was drawn up close to the fire and supper was spread for two, a little impromptu meal of oysters and cake and fruit, but Mr. Stansfield protested that he had dined, and only poured himself out a glass of wine and stood upon the hearth drinking it slowly, whilst with calm interest he watched Virginia. From the platform of his older years, to which he had attained by many struggles and through many disappointments, he looked down with a sort of melancholy wonder at the fearless confidence of youth.

'And yet it is good to be young,' thought Mr. Stansfield.

'Do have a peach,' said Virginia, breaking in upon his meditations. She turned her fair face towards him and stretched out her arm. The fruit lay in her soft palm and his fingers touched hers as he took it from her. 'I am longing to make you some return for your hospitality, and you will not share it with me. But for you I should have gone supperless to bed.'

'Do you think that you will not be able to repay me?'

'Some day, perhaps,' she answered, becoming suddenly serious.

'And how?' he inquired, looking amused.

'That I do not know, but if I can I will help you.'

'Is that a promise? Are you not afraid that I may hold you to it?'

'I always keep my promises!' and she looked a little hurt.

'I am sure of it,' he said, quickly, 'and I will not forget it. You are quite right; some day I may need and may ask your help.'

There is something touching and even humbling in a defence which springs instinctively from inexperience. Its powerlessness inspires reverence. When a child's soft hand is raised to ward off your enemy's blow, your impulse is to snatch it aside and cover it with kisses. Mr. Stansfield knew that he had a difficult part to play; he would allow Virginia to run no risks upon his account, and yet he was surprised and pleased by her spontaneous allegiance.

'And are you not coming back to the drawing-room?' she asked.

'I cannot to-night. These,' laying his hand upon some papers, 'will keep me up long after you are asleep.'

'You work too hard,' observed Virginia,

shaking her head. 'In this family things do not seem to be rightly divided. Hartley has all the play.'

'Such as it is,' he said, a little contemptuously. 'I am not sure that I should find it amusing.'

'Well, good-night,' she said, smiling as she held out her hand. 'Good-night, and thank you for my supper.'

He opened the door for her and closed it again. Then he sat down at his writing-table and busied himself with his accounts, but the room seemed rather darker than usual and more solitary.

Mrs. Stansfield was too wise to take any notice of Virginia's re-appearance. There was music going on at one end of the room, and, under its cover, people were conversing together somewhat loudly. Virginia slipped into a corner by the window and sat down, too unconscious to be shy and well content to be a spectator. Behind her head were drawn the thick, soft folds

of a crimson curtain ; in her hand she held
a spray of stephanotis which she had
gathered as she passed through the conservatory.

'I hope you feel better?' whispered
Hartley, as he seated himself beside her
with an air calculated, as he imagined, to
inspire confidence. He felt himself well
qualified to play the part of a confidant.

'I feel a good deal better,' she answered
aloud, in no wise sharing his desire for a
tête-à-tête.

'In spite of having missed your dinner?'

'I had a very good substitute for dinner,'
answered Virginia, laughing.

'And now you are happy again?'

'I am.'

'Does that assertion need no qualifica-
tions?'

'What a cold-blooded question!' said
the girl, smiling. 'What happiness will
stand being so closely interrogated? Mine
at least abjures your criticisms. If you

must ask such questions, ask them of yourself.'

'They are easily answered. *If* I had a good deal more money, *if* my young brother Jack were not coming home from school next week, and *if* I could sit by you for the rest of the evening, I should be happy,' cried Hartley, whose compliments were apt to be of the most unveiled character.

'Then one element of your happiness will be at once removed,' answered Virginia, a little coldly. 'I see Emmeline is wanting me;' and she rose, and crossed the room to her cousin's side.

'Oh, dear. I am so dreadfully tired,' sighed Miss Stansfield. 'It is too bad of you and Hartley to sit in a corner together. He is always selfish, but I think you might exert yourself to talk to some of these people.'

'Would they like it?'

'It is not a question of what one likes.

If it were, I should be in bed at this moment.'

'You are in request, Miss Tennant.' Captain Damer came up, pleased at the opportunity of seeking her again. 'Will you not sing or play? We were deprived of the pleasure of your company at dinner. Will you not now make us some amends?'

'If it were in my power, but, unluckily, I am no musician;' and, as he took back her refusal to the group round the piano, she added, in a lower tone, to her cousin, 'I see an old lady by the fire, who seems rather left out. I will go and try to amuse her.'

'What will she do next?' sighed Miss Stansfield to herself. 'She has actually gone to be kind to the old Dowager Lady Mainwaring, who thinks it a great condescension to dine here at all, and would like to examine everyone's pedigree before they are introduced to her!'

Virginia had seated herself by the old

lady, and apparently had found no difficulty in making her acquaintance, for she was saying, graciously :

'And so you are Colonel Tennant's only child. I remember him perfectly. He was a very handsome boy, only too languid, and indifferent to society. And he never recovered his spirits after your mother's death, you know, but went and buried himself in France. And where is he now, my dear.'

'In Egypt.'

'Ah! poor child, that is a pity ; and,' turning a pair of sharp, but not unkindly eyes upon her, 'who is taking care of you in his absence.'

'I am staying here with my aunt,' answered Virginia, 'till . . . till he comes back. My old governess is with me.'

'And no one else ! Depend upon it, that woman will have some designs upon her,' muttered the old lady to herself, but so that Virginia could not catch the words.

Then aloud: 'Emmeline Stansfield is such an invalid, or rather so accustomed to imagine herself one, that you cannot have much companionship.' She paused, and looked round to see that no one was near, and then she drew a little closer to the girl, and laid one of her thin old hands, with the diamonds glittering on them, upon her knees. 'My dear,' she said, 'I knew your father well. He was a nice boy. You have something of his smile. Take an old woman's warning. Do not have anything to do with your cousin Hartley. As to the other, he lives almost entirely apart from the rest. He will not trouble you. Don't answer me. I do not wish you to commit yourself; only some day, when the time comes, you may remember my warning.'

Virginia opened her blue eyes a little wider, but they still had the smile in them which reminded Lady Mainwaring of her father's. She thought that she was a kind old lady, but she had strange ideas. What harm could Hartley do her? She was not at all afraid of him.

'Mademoiselle Joseph is always warning me,' she said, smiling, 'of many unknown dangers, but I am afraid she cannot get me to believe in them.'

'Then this Mademoiselle Joseph is a faithful guardian. I am sure of it. But if ever you need another friend come to me. I live only a few miles off. Remember, my dear, that I shall always be glad to see you.'

And, as Virginia thanked her, she went sweeping across the room, in her rich lace and diamonds, to wish Mrs. Stansfield a cold good-night.

CHAPTER VII.

'How many wishes have been whispered above this well! Where have they gone to, I wonder,' said Virginia to herself. In the courtyard at Stansfield, amongst other relics of the past, there was a long disused spring, sacred in other days to the service of youth and love. For who but youth has courage to interrogate the future? who but love asks anything at its hands?

On the rough steps which led down to it, Virginia was standing this morning; eager to fulfil all the conditions which ancient custom had attached to the sure propitiation of the fates. Old Janson, the gardener, had told her all about it.

He had never known anyone to be disappointed who, in good faith, had used the charmed water. When the midday sun at its height sent a faint glimmer of light upon its dark surface, whoever should first raise some water in their right hand and thrice touch their lips to it, should most surely attain their heart's desire.

The sun was already high in the heavens. The young girl, resting one hand upon the low wall, leaned lightly forward with her eyes fixed upon the pool below. The sunlight already quivered in the ferns which sprang from the crevices of the stone-work and on the red hooded threads of the delicate mosses which had done their best to disguise its natural inequalities. Another moment and a shaft like an arrow pierced and, as it were, divided the blackness of the water. Virginia stepped down to its very edge, and, kneeling on the wet and slippery stair, bent over the well, too dull a mirror to reflect even her fairness.

'Once, twice, thrice,' she whispered. The cold water trickled through her fingers, but not before she had for the third time touched her lips to it. She stood up, lifted her broad straw hat which she had laid aside, and lightly shook the drops from her fingers.

'May I ask what incantations you have been practising?' asked Mr. Stansfield's voice.

He had been passing through the court-yard towards a door which opened upon it from his part of the house, and now stood a few paces behind her, arrested on his way by curiosity as to her movements.

'I have only been making a proper use of this wishing-well which you are so fortunate to possess,' answered Virginia, looking, however, for the first time slightly disconcerted.

'And, pray, who told you that it was a wishing-well?'

'Janson and Martin and several others.'

She looked down at the ribbons of her hat
which she was passing through her fingers.
' I suppose you do not believe in it.'

' On the contrary, far be it from me
rashly to impugn so good an authority.
A wishing-well is an heir-loom of which we
may well be proud.   It is a sort of guaran-
tee that one's ancestors lived in the ages of
faith.   If I have never put its virtues to a
practical test, it may be because the fates
are so chary of their favours that they
only allow one a single wish.   Under those
circumstances, the difficulties of choice
would be amply sufficient to keep one
silent.'

' But why ?   I do not understand.'

' Then let us take an illustration,' he said,
seating himself on the stone wall and
casting a pebble carelessly into the water.
' Think of wishing for perpetual youth to
find oneself alone in the world with decay,
age, and disease all round about one; think
of riches without health; think' (smiling) 'of

the old woman and the black pudding in
the fairy tale; think of King Midas, and
beware how you tempt the fates.'

'I am not afraid,' cried Virginia. 'I
have wished for one thing that can bring
me nothing but good.'

'Is it something which you want very
much?'

'It is.'

She clasped her hands tightly together,
and the colour rose in her cheeks whilst
her wet eyes met his.

'You are very happy,' he said, gravely.
'Very happy to be so sure that something
which you may obtain will make you so.'

'Oh, it must come,' she said, looking at
him earnestly, 'it *must* come; but I wish
that it could be quickly.'

'Then I could be unwise enough to echo
your wish,' he answered.

When he left her, she put on her hat
and went out into the sunshine of the
south garden. It had been a mild autumn;

the borders were still bright with holly-
hocks and dahlias, some late roses blos-
somed in a sheltered corner; against
the blue line of the low horizon the woods
spread their gay and varied foliage. Virginia paced the straight walks with her
head bent and her eyes on the gravel.
' He could not know what my wish was,
and he never asked,' she was thinking to
herself; well aware that it would have
needed a strong motive to have restrained
her from questions under similar circumstances. ' I suppose Mr. Stansfield has
other things to think of,' thought Virginia.

'What a lovely morning!' observed
Hartley, coming to meet her. Then, after a
moment's pause: ' Do you know why I have
come home so early?'

It was his habit to leave the house after
breakfast, returning only in time for dinner. He was reading with a tutor about
three miles off, with whom the interme-
diate hours were ostensibly spent; and,

though Mr. Stansfield was not alone in his opinion that he contrived to enliven his studies by companions and pursuits which by no means tended to edification, his mother was powerless and no one else was qualified to control him. Like many other amiable people, he pursued his own way in peace undisturbed by any regard for others.

' Do you know why I have come home so early ?' he repeated.

' No ; how should I know ?' she answered, carelessly. Hartley's comings and goings were of no consequence to her, and she was at no pains to disguise it.

' It is because I see so little of you generally,' answered the young man. ' When I come in you are always shut up with your Mademoiselle Joseph, and after dinner . . .'

' You go to play billiards,' interrupted Virginia, smiling.

Hartley felt that she was taking an

unfair advantage. His mother had told him that he was to make love to this girl, and he was quite prepared to carry out her wishes if they could be accomplished without any great inconvenience to himself. He liked Virginia, but he liked his billiards and his cigars, and the companions of whom his mother disapproved, even better. He liked an easy life and did not take the trouble to hate anyone, unless it were perhaps his half-brother; he was therefore surely entitled to the kindness and consideration of other people. And Virginia was very bright and pretty, but he did not think that she was very kind to him. She gave him no encouragement; if he did slip away from the drawing-room after dinner it was not her place to notice it. At any rate, he had done as his mother wished, he had come home on purpose to invite her to go for a drive with him to-day.

'You are always reading or talking to

my mother or Emmeline in the evening,'
he said, apologetically.

'And why not?' answered Virginia,
opening her blue eyes, apparently altogether unconscious of any apology being
required.

'Well! I don't exactly know why not;
only it must be very dull for you sometimes.   If you would let me teach you to
play billiards or bezique it might amuse
you.'

'Do you think so?' said Virginia, doubtfully.   She had picked one of the late
blossoming roses as they passed, and was
fastening it into her dress.   'But I have
not felt dull as yet.'

'That is because it is all new to you,
but, now that the dark winter days are
coming on, you will find that Emmeline's
headaches will grow worse; and—my
mother is not naturally fond of girls—you
will have no resource . . .' he paused for a
word.

'No resource but billiards and bezique!' said Virginia, laughing.

'I did not mean to say that,' he cried, almost piqued into anger. 'You know quite well that I wished to find some way of telling you that I should like to make you happy here.'

'That is a very kind wish, and I thank you for it.' She stood for a moment in the path and shook her head back with a smile which said, as plainly as if she had spoken, 'But my happiness does not depend upon you, Mr. Hartley Stansfield.' Hartley felt that she was decidedly hard upon him, and yet he persevered.

'Will you come for a drive with me after luncheon,' he said, persuasively. 'The country is very pretty, and it will be a lovely afternoon.'

She hesitated for a moment and then she said,

'I will, if you will order the high dog-cart.   I like to feel myself so high up above the hedges.'

' It shall be ready at three o'clock.'

But though she had acceded to his request he could not feel that he had gained any advantage.   The high dog-cart was evidently more of an object to her than his society.   Frank and unembarrassed though she was, he began to perceive that her intimacy was not to be easily acquired.   Her freedom was the freedom of a branch tossed lightly in the air above your head which ever eludes your grasp.

'Virginia is the most difficult girl in the world,' he said to his mother.

' If you find her so, it must be your own fault,' she answered, with severity.   ' She is not shy, she is not proud, she is not preoccupied.'

' And I admit, my dear mother, that she is very charming.   But that does not interfere with the truth of my assertion, that she is not the least like other girls.'

'Would you have her fashioned after the ordinary type, with no originality, nothing to distinguish her from others?'

'I hardly know.' He hesitated and stroked his slight moustache. 'You see, I am not at all original myself. I do not understand it. Of course,' returning to his first idea. 'Of course I know she is a very charming girl.'

'And you are going to marry her.'

It was a command rather than an interrogation. Mrs. Stansfield shut up her blotting-book with decision, and turned her eyes upon her son. She felt like a skilled workman compelled to use a weak and untrustworthy instrument.

'You can always attain an object if you will keep it steadily in view,' she asserted. 'You are going to marry her.'

Hartley sauntered to the fireplace and

looked at his fair boyish face in the old mirror above it.

'You must ask Virginia,' he said smiling. Mrs. Stansfield was too much annoyed to speak, and Emmeline glancing up from her book broke in upon the conversation.

'I am sure I do not see why Virginia should marry you. I do not believe she will. I cannot for my part see what you have to recommend you.'

'I have my mother,' replied her brother, with perfect good humour, now leaving the contemplation of himself in the glass and dawdling across the room to look out of the window. 'And we must take care of Virginia. We must not allow her to see any other young men.'

'I do not believe that Virginia cares about being married,' persisted Emmeline. 'She is a perfect child in such things.'

'So am I,' observed Hartley. 'I think we should suit each other very well. She might do worse.'

Mrs. Stansfield turned away with an impatient sigh. Her affections and her hopes alike were centred in her son. Emmeline had always been more or less of a perplexity and anxiety to her, and Jack her schoolboy trod on the trains of her dresses and spoilt her carpets with his muddy boots; even as a baby, he had been uproarious and exacting, a very dangerous inmate of any well-regulated household; she felt that Jack's existence was a mistake, but from the very first she had been proud of Hartley. He bore her own maiden name; even as a child, he had gentle little ways of obtaining his own ends; his collars were never rumpled, for the good reason that he never fought with anyone bigger than himself; his somewhat delicate health was an excuse for his never bringing home any prizes or making progress in his studies; and it was only by slow and painful degrees that Mrs. Stansfield had become aware of his deficiencies. Her influence was not sufficiently powerful to remedy them, but marriage and prosperity might yet do much. Virginia seemed to Mrs. Stansfield to have been sent to her exactly at the right moment; it only remained for Hartley himself to make a good use of his opportunities.

'Do not look so melancholy, my dear mother,' cried Hartley. 'Am I not doing my best to carry out your wishes. I have persuaded her to let me take her for a *tête-à-tête* drive this afternoon, and,' persuasively, 'if you will give me some money, I will buy her a present.'

But his mother was too wise to advance him anything upon this hypothesis, and Emmeline hastened to assure him that Virginia would certainly not accept anything from him.

'Then that proves my point. She is not the least like other girls. That is why it is so hard to please her.'

'But Emmeline is right, she is so easily pleased,' cried Mrs. Stansfield. 'She is a child to be delighted with a word of praise, a toy, a holiday.'

'Only unfortunately, my dear mother, children do not care about lovers.'

He was confirmed in his opinion during their drive that afternoon. Virginia was sufficiently gracious, but she was not communicative nor did she give him any opportunity for making the most of their *tête-à-tête*. She was even a little preoccupied and graver that usual. When they reached home she did not come into the drawing-room for tea, but went straight upstairs to her own room.

'It must come. I feel that it will come to-night,' she said; and she went and knelt down by Mademoiselle Joseph, and laid her head upon her shoulder. She was trembling with excitement. The old Frenchwoman put aside her book and her spectacles, and took the girl's cold hands in hers. 'No one cares for him but you, I could not tell anyone else—but I—I can-

not bear this silence any longer;' and there
was a sob in her voice. Only that morning she had passed singing down the passages, and full of hope had bent her head
in the sunlight over the wishing-well!
But she was right, when one is young it is
impossible to be always unhappy. Mademoiselle Joseph's thin fingers pressed hers
gently. She said nothing. She knew that
Virginia spoke of the letter from her father
which as yet had never come, and now
that it had been so long delayed her old
friend dreaded the news which it might
bring. There are times when one would not
exchange a fear for a certainty. Mademoiselle Joseph, who under all circumstances
looked for the worst, had no comfort to
give.

The hall at Stansfield was a square one
with a great fire-place at one end of it, and
two doors opening into the drawing-room
and dining-room facing the staircase. On
a marble-table between these doors the

evening letters were laid, and as Mr. Stansfield came down the stairs he saw Virginia
standing before this table. She was still in
her morning-dress, and she held an un-
opened letter in her hands.

'I *dare* not open it,' she cried, in a low
voice, as she turned at the sound of his
step upon the stones. The colour had fled
from her cheeks, under the excitement of
the moment, and her eyes looked dark.
'I have been waiting for it so long. I
cannot tell what it may say. I said the
fulfilment of my wish could only bring me
happiness, but you were right to warn me.
Oh! I dare not look at it.'

Mr. Stansfield set down his candle on
the table beside her, and glanced at the
letter which she held.

'I feel sure that it is good news,' he
said, kindly. 'See how strong and firm
the hand-writing is. Believe me you
need not be afraid to break the seal.
Your father is safe and well. Will you

come into the library, you can read it there in peace?'

He led the way across the hall, and lifted the curtain which hung over the archway to let her pass. But the room was in partial darkness. The servants had forgotten to light the lamp, only the wood fire crackled and blazed upon the hearth. Whilst Mr. Stansfield lighted the candles above the chimney-piece, Virginia knelt upon the rug, and with cold and trembling fingers opened her letter.

'You are right,' she cried, after an instant's pause. 'How right you are! He is safe and well. He would not deceive me even to make me happy. This is worth all the fear and the waiting.' The tears were running down her cheeks as she kissed the signature at the bottom of the page.

Mr. Stansfield stood silent looking down at her, but she had for the moment forgotten his presence. He was interested, but, more than that, he was surprised. An affection at once so deep and so unreserved had never before come within the range of his experience. He did not know that the girl's nature, though under some aspects proud and reticent, would open beneath the influence of kindness as naturally as a flower opens to the sun.

'What a good prophet you were!' Virginia looked up at him with a smile upon her parted lips. 'He thinks that he may very likely be at home by next year.'

'And you will go back to him?'

'Yes; I shall go back to him of course,' she echoed, with unfeigned satisfaction.

'Your thoughts ever turn southward. You would leave us, if you might, with the swallows.'

'I would not be ungrateful,' she answered, quietly. 'It is very kind of Mrs. Stansfield to have me here.'

He was silent; but glancing at him she perceived that it was not the silence of acquiescence.

'But it is kind of her,' she persisted. 'She does not like girls; Hartley told me she did not.'

'I would advise you to take his assertions with some reserve.'

'I generally believe what I am told,' answered Virginia, seriously, 'until I find out for myself that people are not to be trusted. You see, I believed in you this evening, I believed in the wishing-well, and I was not mistaken,' clasping her letter more tightly. 'I was not mistaken.'

'But then we both prophesied good and not evil. If I ever foretell any but blessings for you, may I be no true prophet.'

He spoke lightly, yet his look was grave and even a little melancholy.

'When once I have papa back again you may prophesy what you please,' cried Virginia, rising to her feet. 'I shall not be afraid of anything then. Nothing else can matter to me—nothing.'

Mr. Stansfield remained alone standing over the fire; he looked thoughtful and preoccupied. 'And so a woman ever risks her all upon one plank,' he was thinking; 'she would not be so far wrong if it were indeed true that love is enough, but a good many other things go to make up the sum of life. May this poor child never stake her all and lose.' Then he thought of her absolute unconsciousness as she knelt at his feet and kissed the letters of the beloved name. 'Why should she love him so much? I remember Colonel Tennant perfectly, he is a gentleman, and he has many amiable qualities ; but it is an infinite pity that she should love him like that. She is making a terrible mistake. Of course he will be killed or die of fever, and then what will become of the girl?'

He could not answer the question. He extinguished the lights and joined the rest of the party in the drawing-room.

CHAPTER VIII.

MRS. STANSFIELD was in her private sitting-room with account-books and ledgers upon the table before her. She had been writing and making notes with a business-like air of decision. Mr. Marshall the steward had been assisting at her deliberations, and he was just about to take his leave.

'But if Mr. Norton . . .' he suggested in his insinuating, deferential voice.

'It will not be necessary to speak to Mr. Norton,' answered his step-mother. Yet as Marshall left the room she remained buried in thought with a harassed look upon her face. No instinct of high breeding stepped in to make the confederacy of her steward distasteful to her. It was not the first time that she had stooped to underhand measures to do her step-son an injury, but she began to fear that these petty persecutions would never drive him from Stansfield. Now the fates had put a new weapon in her hands. It would be hard if she could not succeed in marrying a young girl placed in her sole charge, unguarded and unwarned, to a young man who in her maternal eyes had much to recommend him. Hartley married to Colonel Tennant's rich daughter would be in a very different position from that which he now occupied with regard to his elder brother. She herself would be in a measure freed from a state of enforced dependence. She felt as if fortune's wheel were about to turn, and it only needed a light and secret pressure from her hand to move it in the right direction.

Virginia was too inexperienced; Norton,

even if he happened to take an interest in the girl, would be too proud to oppose her; her chief trouble was that she was not sure of Hartley. She might work herself to death in his service, and he would not hold out a helping hand if it cost him a single luxury or a day's enjoyment. She sighed impatiently as she thought of him, and then her meditations reverted to Virginia. She at least need give her but little anxiety. She had lived such a solitary life that it was not possible her affections should be already engaged, and she would be certain to be flattered by Hartley's admiration, and prepared to accept his proposals. Fortunately that curious dilapidated old governess could not be supposed to have any influence, still it might be prudent to engage her as an ally; and, having arrived at this conclusion, Mrs. Stansfield, for the first time, voluntarily sought her in her own apartments.

Mademoiselle Joseph was somewhat

bewildered by the honour done to her.
She rose to the full height of her angular
figure, and, letting her wools and canvas
fall to the ground, offered the arm-chair in
which she had been seated to Mrs. Stansfield. Mrs. Stansfield accepted it graciously, signing to the governess to place herself
in an opposite chair, and then after sundry
preambles opened the campaign. She was
sure that Virginia came first in Mademoiselle Joseph's thoughts; she was persuaded that she had her true interests at
heart. Mademoiselle Joseph inclined her
head in grave assent, but did not commit
her thoughts to speech.

'I too,' continued Mrs. Stansfield, with
a sigh, 'feel much anxiety about the poor
child's future.'

Mademoiselle Joseph cast an inquiring
glance in her direction, but still remained
silent.

'I should be thankful, my dear Mademoiselle Joseph, to see her in good hands.

Colonel Tennant's life is naturally a precarious one, and I should desire nothing better than to keep her altogether with me; but under existing circumstances you may well understand that motives of delicacy might forbid this.'

'I am not sure, madame, that I under-stand your meaning.', Mademoiselle Joseph's manner was deprecating, but it was also watchful. She felt, for some unknown reason, suspicious of Mrs. Stansfield's advances.

'Shall I make it plain? I would not admit as much to others, but I can have no secrets from you, Virginia's oldest friend. I have two young men in the house, mademoiselle, my stepson and my son.'

Even Mademoiselle Joseph's simplicity perceived that this fact, in the nature of things, could not well be a secret from anyone. She made no comment upon it.

'Virginia, as you know, has good expectations,' continued Mrs. Stansfield, ' and Mr. Norton Stansfield is, unfortunately, aware of them. He is a man of the world, and he makes no secret of a wish to improve his position by a wealthy marriage. I confess to you, Mademoiselle Joseph, that, if I had known what I know now, I should have hesitated to offer Virginia a home at Stansfield. Most unhappily, he is not a man to whom one would entrust a young girl's happiness.'

Mademoiselle Joseph moved restlessly upon her chair and twisted her long fingers nervously together. She was distrustful of Mrs. Stansfield, but upon this one point she agreed with her.

' Now Hartley has his faults,' said Mrs. Stansfield, candidly. ' I should be the last to deny it. I am always inclined to be hard upon him, poor boy. But he is so affectionate and reliable that though of course I should dread any entanglement at his age, at some future time I should

consider the girl of his affections to be en-
vied. He is a safe companion for our dear
Virginia, and too much of a boy to have at
present any thought of love or marriage.

ut you see my position, my dear Mademoiselle Joseph. I am bound in honour
to defend her from any advances on the
part of my own son; I am still more bound
by my affection for her to save her from
any designs of Mr. Norton Stansfield.'

'Virginia is still very young,' faltered the
poor Frenchwoman, still cautious in spite of
her perturbation of spirit. 'She has had
no experience in these matters. Her heart
is untouched and her fancy free. Why
should it not remain so?'

'Because in the nature of things it is
impossible,' answered Mrs. Stansfield, somewhat impatiently. 'She is young, but she
is very pretty and eminently attractive.
She has none of the shyness or awkwardness
of a school-girl. She is well able to take
her place in society, and sooner or later for

better or for worse she will love and be loved.'

' You are right ; it is the common fate,' sighed Mademoiselle Joseph, who felt her arguments to be unanswerable.

' And Virginia will certainly not escape from it. I trust to you in her father's absence, mademoiselle, to join with me in protecting her from the designs of . . of . . improper persons, and I imagine that Hartley, who merely looks upon her as a favourite cousin, will be our best ally.'

Mademoiselle Joseph drew herself up a little stiffly.

' I shall do my best to prove deserving of the confidence which Colonel Tennant has shown in me,' she said, proudly. She would say no more. She did not trust Mrs. Stansfield any the better for her smooth speeches. She agreed with her; she had no liking for Mr. Norton Stansfield, at the same time she was not prepared to encourage Hartley's attentions.   ' If

Virginia is not too young to be loved, he is not too young to love,' she said, shrewdly to herself. Mademoiselle Joseph was, after all, capable of drawing her own conclusions.

Stansfield was somewhat dull that autumn. There were not many country neighbours, and those whom there were visited the house but seldom. Mrs. Stansfield averred that it was difficult for her to receive people when Norton persisted in holding aloof, and yet occupied the position of the master of the house. Hartley provided himself with pleasures and companions whom he did not care to introduce to his family, and Emmeline during these dark wintry days lay wrapped up with furs upon her knees. Mrs. Stansfield, who had many letters to write and much business to transact with Marshall, contributed little to the enlivenment of the party; and Mr. Stansfield was frequently absent from home. Virginia kept more and more to her own little sitting-room upstairs, which with its stand of flowers, its bright hangings and the wood fire blazing on the tiled hearth, was always a cheerful abode. It was there that she read the books she had abstracted on various occasions from the library; it was there that she wrote long letters to her father, or sat over her embroidery whilst the old Frenchwoman read aloud to her. That little room was like a spot of sunshine in a darkened place; but for that, the old house would have been gloomy enough. Yet Virginia was not dispirited. She had been used to a tranquil existence and she did not weary of it; only at times she missed the affection which she had imagined would have been naturally accorded to her. She would have received it as a gift not as a right; nevertheless, she felt herself to be defrauded.

'They do not care for me,' she said to Mademoiselle Joseph. 'But what does that matter so long as I have papa's love, and yours;' and she pressed her young soft cheek caressingly against that of the old Frenchwoman. 'I do not think that I need more to keep my heart warm. If no one else loves me, it will not make me unhappy.'

'Ah! if you could but think so always,' cried Mademoiselle Joseph. 'These calm affections of relationship and long usage are indeed as you say a fire, which warms but which will never devastate.'

Virginia looked thoughtful for a moment, and then a half-mocking smile flashed across her face.

'This little cheerful wood fire in the grate is very pleasant,' she said, 'but a wild rushing prairie fire must be a fine sight, Mademoiselle Joseph.'

'At a distance perhaps you may be right,' she answered, hardly understanding Virginia's ready adoption of her metaphor. 'But it is very unwise to approach such too nearly.'

'And you and I are in no danger, are we?' cried the girl, laughing.

It was growing a little dusk. This was the hour when tea was brought into the drawing-room, and the members of the family met for a little intercourse, often so brief and interrupted as to be bereft of its sociable character. Mrs. Stansfield from her writing-table would decline tea altogether. Emmeline would draw a little table to her side, and after making various arrangements for her comfort, subside again into silence and her book. As for Mr. Stansfield, it was rarely that he appeared at all at this hour; and when he came he would stand for a few minutes on the rug, take his cup of tea from his sister's hands, and return again to the library. Virginia on her part had no liking for the drawing-room; the indifference and silence with which she was greeted oppressed her spirits and irritated her temper; she too sought it unwillingly, and left it gladly.

This evening, on her way, she lingered by the hall fire. Her feet sank into the thick fur of the rug before it, as she spread out her hands to the glowing warmth. She smiled a little to herself. 'This is not worth very much, but it is worth something,' she thought. 'Mrs. Stansfield's roof shelters me, her fire warms me! I am fed at her table. Is it not ungrateful to ask for anything more?'

The drawing-room door was ajar, and the voices within fell upon her ear; but she paid no heed to them, she was lost in her own reflections. Her own name recalled her to the present.

'I tell you that Virginia is not difficult to approach,' Mrs. Stansfield was saying, in a somewhat raised and indignant voice. 'But you will take no trouble whatever about the matter. You expect the fruit to drop into your mouth. If you would interest her, talk to her, devote yourself . . .'

Virgina's first thought was to beat a

hasty retreat; but indignation got the better of prudence. She walked into the drawing-room, with a quick light step, and closed the door behind her. Her aunt was seated with her face turned towards Hartley, who stood by the fire looking a little bored, and a little sheepish, like a boy who has been receiving a lecture. Virginia came in and stood between them; she glanced at him for an instant, and then she addressed herself to his mother.

'I am very sorry that you should have been finding fault with Hartley upon my account, Aunt Charlotte,' she said, calmly, but with heightened colour. 'It was very kind of you to ask me to Stansfield, but it would be impossible for me to stay here if anyone were to be made unhappy or inconvenienced.'

'My dear child, you misunderstood; you did not allow me to finish my sentence. You made a mistake,' cried Mrs. Stansfield, stumbling in her endeavour to recover the false step she had taken.

'I could not make a mistake,' answered Virginia, with unruffled self-possession. 'I could not help hearing what you said. Only do not reprove Hartley again upon my account, it would not please him, and it would vex me . . .'

'He has a defender then in you.'

'He has,' answered Virginia, smiling, 'when reproofs addressed to him happen to recoil upon me.'

'Then your motives are purely selfish.'

'Yes, purely selfish!' echoed Virginia, smiling again, and going to the table to pour herself out a cup of tea.

'Do you know, I am not sure that I should care to be defended upon those terms,' observed her cousin, following her and speaking in rather a lower tone.

'That is unfortunate,' she answered, in-differently, 'as they are the only terms upon which you will be likely to secure me as an ally.'

'But in this case . . .' he persisted.

'In this case,' she interrupted, impatiently, 'I was especially called upon to defend you; if you had happened to take your mother's reproofs to heart, it would have been decidedly inconvenient for me.'

'I cannot see why you should be so determined to keep me at a distance,' he continued, in a melancholy voice. 'You are not unsociable.'

'Not at all,' cried Virginia, cheerfully.

'You are not shy?'

'No; I am not shy of *you*, certainly,' with a decided but not ill-natured emphasis.

'You are my cousin.'

'I am.   I do not deny it.'

'You are not proud, surely?'

'Ah, you have hit upon the true explanation at last,' cried Virginia, looking at him over the edge of her tea-cup with a gleam of laughter in her eyes. 'I am proud. Too proud to be indebted to you for courtesies and attentions which you offer to me at your mother's command, Mr. Hartley Stansfield.'

'But if I could persuade you to the contrary. If you knew that they were offered in all sincerity, but so sparingly, so rarely only because I feared to offend you ; if . . .'

'Stay!' cried Virginia, a little shortly ; 'do not let us suppose anything so improbable. I am entirely in accord with you upon one point. I am your cousin, be satisfied with that ; it is a relationship which has many advantages, do not forfeit them.'

She put down her cup and turned from him with a little air of not unkind decision, and went and sat down at the end of Emmeline's couch. Miss Stansfield's worn face looked sadder and less fretful than usual. She was always pale, and the fair hair cut

in a straight line across her forehead could
not shadow or soften her sharp refined
features.　She held a book listlessly half-
opened in the thin hand which hung over
the edge of the sofa.

'What is it?' asked Virginia, gently.
Her fresh and deeper colouring threw her
cousin's pallor into strong contrast.

'It is so hopeless;' and for the moment
the cynical tone had gone out of Miss
Stansfield's voice. 'It is a physical weakness against which it is useless to strive,
and all the while I know that I might have
been able to understand.' She paused,
and her faint eyes which were so often
clouded by pain sought Virginia's face. 'I
never cared for anything else.　I never
wanted health or strength except as
means to an end, but I did wish to be
clever, and now I begin to see that it is
hopeless.　I cannot understand any better,
perhaps not so well as I did two years
ago.'

She lifted the book she held and laid it down with a sigh.

Virginia opened it again and glanced at the page.

'But this is horribly difficult,' she cried, very sincerely. 'Such long words and involved sentences. I think you are very clever indeed to be able to read a single page.'

'You could not understand it?'

'Most certainly not.'

'Yet it does not distress you?'

'Why should it?' cried Virginia, laughing. 'I am not . . .' she stopped, blushing.

'Were you going to say that you are not clever?' asked Emmeline, looking at her curiously. 'Pray finish your sentence. I daresay you are quite right. You need not mind. People who can manage to be happy do not need anything more.'

Virginia looked at her for a moment in silence, and then she laughed with perfect good humour.

'Perhaps I shall find my level at Stansfield. I think I have learnt something already.'

'What do you mean?'

'There was no tree of knowledge in the Eden of La Vallière,' answered the girl, gravely.

CHAPTER IX.

It was a dull November day. The sky had the peculiar leaden look which precedes a fall of snow; the dead leaves, heavy and limp from late rains, lay thickly upon the ground; down in the hollows the pools were edged with ice; and the river ran in a swift dark current through the wet grass. Even Virginia's spirits were oppressed by the dull and threatening atmosphere. She shivered a little as she walked alone in the garden. As naturally as an exile's thoughts turn in hours of despondency to the land of his birth, so hers fled at this moment to a foreign shore. 'If I could only see him but for one moment and hear him say that

he was well;' she sighed, and the tears
gathered in her eyes, but the piercing wind
dried them before they had time to fall.
She shook back her head a little impatiently,
as if to rid herself of such gloomy imagina-
tions, and re-entered the house. She could
no longer bear the chill depression of the
outer air, and yet she wished to be alone.
She dreaded Mademoiselle Joseph's questions even more than the unsympathetic
conversation of her aunt or cousins. She
had of late seen Mr. Stansfield so rarely
that she had become shy of encountering
him by chance, and as he was to return
home from one of his brief absences that
day she would not take refuge in the
library. The dining-room, however, was
certain to be untenanted. She opened
the door, and as she closed it again behind
her thought she heard a sound as of a soft
scuffle on the Turkey carpet; but the room
she saw by the uncertain light was empty
and in decorous order, the chairs ranged

against the walls and round the dinner table upon which the cloth and glasses were placed ready for dinner. The heavy window curtains obscured the last struggling rays of daylight.

The fire itself was dull and smouldering. As she knelt down upon the rug and stirred it into a blaze, she seemed to hear again a noise as of some one or something moving close beside her. She grasped the poker more firmly and looked round.

'Who is there? Is anyone there.'

A sort of sound between a stifled groan and suppressed laughter answered her. She started to her feet and felt for the bell, but in the dim light she failed to find it.

'Don't ring,' cried a boy's voice, whilst from under the falling tablecloth a boy's head and shoulders became visible. 'If you don't ring, I won't frighten you any more.'

'You have not frightened me in the least,' answered Virginia, angrily.

'Oh, haven't I?' cried the boy, with an incredulous chuckle, 'I know very well you took me for a ghost or a burglar. Why, you are shaking all over. You are quite right, I have got a jemmy in my pocket, and I have come for the spoons; but if you keep quiet I won't shoot you.'

'Then come out from under the table,' said Virginia, who began to have a suspicion of who he might be. He had Emmeline's features, sharpened not so much by ill-health as by shrewdness; small, inquisitive eyes, a rough, fair head of hair, and a schoolboy's jacket and collar. He emerged upon all fours and sat down upon his heels to stare at her.

'Do you know who I am now?' he inquired.

'You are a very bad boy,' answered Virginia, indignantly, 'and I suppose that

you are Jack.   But everyone, yes, *everyone*,
hoped that you were not coming home till
Christmas.'

'Then for once they were mistaken.
Perhaps you may remember that I was expected a month ago. There was an alarm of
fever and we were going to break up, but
it was a false alarm, or so they said; at any
rate there is no mistake about it this time.'

'What! Have they fever at your school
now?'

'I should rather think they had.   I left
half the boys out of their senses with it.
I'm reeking with it myself.   I have given
it to the cat already.   Her pulse is up to
one hundred and fifty. Mamma and Emmeline won't come within a mile of me.   I'm
in quarantine, you know.   They sent me
up to my bed-room.   That's why I came
in here.   I wasn't going to be stuffed up
in an attic.   I meant to stay until they
came in to dinner, and then jump out
upon them.'

'Then I am very glad that I came in. I shall go and tell your mother of you.'

'You'd better not;' and he at once laid hold of her dress. 'Stop a minute. It is no good your running away now. I'm horribly infectious, and of course I have given it to you already. I'm awfully glad. When I am shut up I shall have some one to keep me company. Can you play bezique?'

Virginia was very young, and she had of late been living in an unnaturally depressed atmosphere; this sudden and unexpected contact with the unreasonable and uncalled-for hilarity of youth brought about a reaction. She sat down on the rug beside her boy-cousin and began to laugh.

'I am sure you must be glad that I have come home, I have cheered you up already,' he observed, looking at her with obvious approbation. 'Only mind, you are not to call me names any more. It is quite a mistake; I am not at all a bad boy. Hartley is the black sheep of the family, and you know there is never more than one in a house.'

Virginia nodded her head. She considered that his judgment of his brother was in the main correct.

'Still, you are a bad boy. It was very unkind of you to have wished to give me scarlet fever; and if I am ill I shall certainly not play with you; besides, I am too old.'

'You are not at all old, and if you are not kind to me you will repent it.'

'I shall be kind to you if you behave yourself. Not if you hide under tables and tell untruths.'

'Well, if I promise not to give you scarlet-fever, you ought to promise me something in return.'

'I shall not promise anything. I shall wait to see how you behave.'

Some one opened the door, and, in an

instant, he had noiselessly retreated again beneath the table. The intruder was Hartley, who was advancing to the side-board when he perceived Virginia.

'How fortunate I am! I had no idea that I should find you here.'

'So I supposed,' she answered, with a slight smile.

'Do not be unkind to-day,' he continued, looking a little injured. 'The weather is enough in itself to make one gloomy, and you can make the sun shine at your will.'

'I wish that I could; but, unfortunately, I am no such magician.'

'How can you say so when you know that one smile from you . . .'

'Come, do not be absurd,' interrupted Virginia, hastily, mindful of the unseen auditor whose presence she was yet un-willing to reveal. 'You know I do not like compliments. I am not sufficiently credulous to accept them.'

‘And yet you like praise.’

‘That is another matter. Sincere praise from those whose opinion one values is, I admit, exhilarating. Compliments, like sweetmeats, are apt to pall upon one. They are like those coloured comfits which have a thin coating of sugar and nothing inside.’

‘But I did not intend to pay you a compliment. I do not know why you should distrust me. It is not quite fair. You know perfectly well that, when you came here, the house became a different place. Even Norton can now be pleasant sometimes.’

‘Can he?’ she questioned, with a flush of pleased surprise.

He looked up, and his boyish face clouded visibly. He was not so inexperienced as his mother would have fain believed, and he perceived that he had made a false step.

'You see, Norton hates us all, and he has not found a good excuse for hating you yet.'

'Does he want one?' asked Virginia, speaking rather to herself than to her cousin; and he thought it best to ignore the question.

'You should not be so pretty and charming, if one is not to be allowed to acknowledge it,' he continued, in a tone of amiable complaint.

She looked a little displeased, and said, with quick impatience,

'Let us seek some more profitable subject for conversation.' Then, relenting, with a smile; 'I can assure you I am well aware of my advantages. Mademoiselle Joseph often tells me that I have too much self-confidence. Her ideal is a *jeune fille bien elevée*—timid, retiring, humble.'

'And you transcend her ideal!'

'On the contrary, these are just the virtues which I do not happen to possess.'

'Then they are unnecessary, or rather, they are well replaced by other and rarer ones. I have known a great many girls, but I have never yet known one who made me feel so unworthy, who could . . .' he broke off suddenly, looking mortified. ' You are not listening.'

'But I am,' cried a sepulchral voice, which seemed to come from the floor.

'Good heavens, what is that?' asked Hartley, startled.

Dead silence answered him. Virginia's eyes were bright with suppressed laughter as she put her finger upon her lips.

'Some one is hidden in the room, and you knew it, Virginia. You might at least have warned if you did not wish to hear me.'

' I beg your pardon,' she answered, getting the better of her laughter, and frankly holding out her hand. 'You know we were not discussing state secrets, and it is only your brother Jack who chose for reasons of his own to secrete himself here. I did not like to betray him.'

'Why, he was to have been shut up in his room for at least a month. I shall go and tell my mother;' and with somewhat suspicious haste he left the room.

'So Hartley wants to make love to you, does he?' cried Master Jack, emerging from under the table almost before his brother was out of the room. 'My eyes, didn't he come a cropper! Unless I could do it a little better, I'd go and take lessons from some one if I were Hartley.'

The girl lifted her head a little haughtily.

'I do not understand you.'

In fact, his phraseology was occasionally unintelligible to her, English slang being an unknown language.

'It was plain enough to see what he was driving at,' he answered, in no wise abashed. 'But you take my advice. Don't have anything to do with Hartley. You

are much too good for him. I know all
about him, and you deserve better things.
You wait till I'm grown up, and I'll do
better for you than that. He is a wolf in
sheep's clothing.'

'And pray what are you?'

'I?' said Jack, winking his eyes and
chuckling. 'I am a sheep in wolf's clothing. You see I did not shoot you or give
you scarlet fever. I am a terror to evil-
doers; but, if you are good to me, you will
find that I am a very lamb. It is too bad
of them to let you be out of spirits. We
will alter all that now I have come home;
only I can't spare you any more time just
now; I must go and give this fever to
some one else. After all, you might find
it slow if you were shut up all alone with
me; besides, I want to see how Hartley
carries on his little game.'

'I think you are very impertinent,' said
Virginia; but she was, as he had said, out

of spirits, and in no mood to carry on the discussion. As she mounted the stairs she met Mrs. Stansfield coming down.

'So you brought Hartley home again this afternoon before his time. We must not allow this. He will be failing in his examination.'

She smiled, and laid her hand affectionately upon the girl's shoulder. Virginia drew back a little.

' I did not know that he had come home earlier than usual, Aunt Charlotte. I had nothing to do with it.'

'Do you think so? Was he not with you just now?'

'Certainly. He came into the dining-room and unexpectedly found me there,' answered the girl, coldly.

'My dear Virginia, how quickly you take up arms! I was not blaming you. I do not grudge my poor boy his *tête-à-tête*, more especially as Norton is coming home this evening.'

'Why, what difference can that make?' asked Virginia, looking puzzled.

'Surely you have observed what a constraint he casts over our little family party. He cannot help it, perhaps. It is the result of constitutional reserve which some people might stigmatize as sullenness; but I really do not think he can control it.'

'I should have thought that Mr. Stansfield had more than his share of self-control,' answered Virginia, coolly.

'It is very necessary that he should exercise it. But I confess that I would almost rather see an occasional ebullition of temper than such moody self-restraint. Some one said the other day that his presence was like a thunder-cloud: one is tempted to wish that it might break.'

'Not on my head!' cried Virginia, smiling, and shaking back the hair from her forehead.

'Poor child, he has already succeeded in making you afraid of him. You are not timid, yet you would be afraid to displease him?'

Virginia paused a moment.

'I should be *sorry* to do so,' she said, softly, and passed slowly up the stairs.

Mrs. Stansfield, like her son, felt dissatisfied. She wished that Virginia had used another word.

For a wonder Mademoiselle Joseph was not alone. She had abdicated in favour of a visitor, and in the high-backed armchair in which she generally sat upright and stiff, Miss Stansfield was seated, with a cushion at her back, resting her small feet upon a high footstool. She was reading French aloud in a monotonous tone, and with her usual air of languor.

'You see, I have invaded your sanctum,' she said, interrupting herself to look up at her cousin. 'Mademoiselle is acting as my dictionary. It was so wearisome to look out words. It is a great shame that they did not manage to teach me all this long ago. I had more governesses than most people. I could have learnt as well as anyone. I was never stupid.'

'Did they all act as your dictionaries?' asked Virginia, smiling.

'Indeed, they were far too lazy,' answered Miss Stansfield. 'They were actually so unreasonable as to expect me to take all the trouble; and of course I could not do that. If you hire a carriage, you do not expect to be asked to get out and draw it. I would not draw and they could not drive, and so we ended by sitting inside the carriage together, and my education was at a standstill.'

'But your accent is so good, my dear Miss Stansfield,' said the polite Frenchwoman. 'You must have had very superior instructors.'

'No, there is not one of us really well educated, unless it is Norton, and he takes good care to keep his knowledge to himself.'

'Mr. Stansfield is somewhat of a recluse?' observed Mademoiselle Joseph.

'He likes solitude, and no one grudges it to him,' answered Emmeline. 'But I wish he would remember that other people besides himself can take pleasure in books. I cannot see,' discontentedly, 'why the library should be forbidden ground. Especially now that he is so much away, it is absurd to keep it for his exclusive use. Some of the most comfortable arm-chairs in the house are there. There is one which exactly fits the curve of my shoulders.'

'Do you mean that low chair covered in green velvet?' asked Virginia. 'You are quite right, it is very luxurious.'

'And pray when did you find that out?'

'One day when I happened to sit in it,' answered Virginia, composedly; but she could not help colouring beneath her cousin's curious gaze, for she remembered perfectly that it was on the evening of

the dinner-party that Mr. Stansfield had
offered it to her with the assurance that
she would find it the most comfortable
chair in the house.

'Virginia often goes to the library for
books,' said Mademoiselle Joseph, inno-
cently.

'Indeed; and you are not afraid of
meeting Norton?'

'He has never given me any reason
to be afraid of him,' answered Virginia.
She stood with her back against the
low mantel-piece, facing her cousin. The
candles were reflected in the old-fashioned
square mirror behind her; the light fell
upon her fair, frank face. 'Why should I
be afraid of anyone? I have never injured anyone. No one would be so unjust
as to wish to harm me.'

'And who is so old-fashioned as still to
believe in justice?' asked Emmeline. 'That
is one of the virtues which has long since
taken flight from the world. Ask Norton

what he thinks of justice when you see him next, Virginia.'

But, like her mother and Hartley, she said to herself that it did not please her that Virginia should see much of her step-brother. He was horribly gloomy and severe; but still one could never be sure of what might happen, and decidedly Virginia could not be judged by ordinary rules. She was not like other girls. If by any chance she were to fall in love with Norton, or he were to fall in love with her, it would be certain to make a disturbance in the household. 'Between them all, they would be sure to make me very uncomfortable,' sighed Miss Stansfield to herself. 'People are so inconsiderate.'

CHAPTER X.

It is a very difficult thing to make love to a girl who is frankly indifferent to you, unless your own affections are very much engaged; and so Hartley Stansfield found it. He liked and admired Virginia; her beauty charmed and her versatility attracted him, but he was not in love with her; and she upon her part was friendly, but beyond that point she absolutely refused to go. She met his most lover-like speeches with laughing incredulity or open disdain.

Christmas was already upon them, and he had made no sort of advance; he had not gained one solitary advantage. He

was too gentle to take even an outpost
by storm; he was not courageous enough
to attack the stronghold. This would not
have disturbed him much, if it had not
been for his mother; but Mrs. Stansfield
felt herself to be justly angered, and she
did not spare him. She had given him
the most agreeable task possible: to win
a pretty and wealthy girl for his wife,
and he listened, hesitated, and refused to
accomplish it. She was persuaded that
it was his own fault. Virginia had no
other attachment, and therefore there
could be no serious obstacle in his way.

'You will never gain anything by your
faint-heartedness,' she said, angrily.

It was a wet afternoon, and Hartley was
alone with her in the big drawing-room.
He had been driven in by the rain, and
sat by the fire listlessly turning over
the leaves of a periodical. Emmeline
was right in saying that none of the
Stansfields were well educated. Hartley

never took up a book except as a last resource.

'I wish I were sure that I should gain by anything else, my dear mother.'

'Have you ever shown her that you really care for her?'

'I suppose so,' he murmured, with his eyes fixed on the fire.

'But how? Have you told her that you wish to win her?'

'I have not proposed to her, if that is what you mean. I thought it would be rather . . . premature.'

'Your proposals are more likely to come too late than too soon. When some one else . . .'

'But, luckily, there is no one else.'

'We cannot keep her here for ever,' answered Mrs. Stansfield, gloomily. 'At any moment her father may be ordered or invalided home. There is no time like the present.'

'*Time*, three o'clock on a wet November

afternoon. *Place*, the little sitting-room upstairs. *Dramatis Personæ*, myself, Virginia, *and* Mademoiselle Joseph. No, my dear mother, I cannot agree with you. The fates are not propitious.'

'Virginia is not upstairs.' Mrs. Stansfield hardly repressed her irritation, which was only apparent in the sharpened tone of her voice. 'She is alone in the conservatory, where you may find her if you will.'

Hartley closed his magazine, and let it slip from his hand; then he stood up, and walked in a dubious manner to the fireplace. He smoothed the hair upon his forehead, as he looked at himself in the glass, and then he turned to his mother.

'She will be certain to refuse me,' he observed, colouring a little.

'That depends in a great measure upon yourself,' answered Mrs. Stansfield, with decision. 'If you are determined to win,

you will do so in the end. You wish to
marry her?'

'I do.   At least, I wish her to marry
me.   I suppose it comes to much the same
thing.'

'I daresay; though it is not a very
manly way of looking at the matter. At
any rate, it is quite certain that she will
not marry you unless you ask her.'

He paused for a moment as if weighing
the question, or perhaps one more difficult
of solution, for he looked flushed and
uneasy.

'Very well, then, you take the responsibility?'

'What! of her refusal?'

'No, of her acceptance!' he cried, 'and
that is a far more serious matter.'

He did not wait for an answer, but left
the room and at once crossed the hall to
the conservatory.

'I have roused him at last!' thought

Mrs. Stansfield, complacently; but she was restless, and could not fix her mind as easily as usual upon her business.

An hour later, Mr. Stansfield, as he sat alone in the library, was disturbed by a knock at the door.

'Come in,' he answered, without lifting his head, as he ran his eye down a column of figures.

'Mr. Stansfield,' said a girl's voice, 'you are the master of this house. You ought to know why I cannot live here any longer.'

She spoke low, but her words fell clear and distinct as notes struck upon an instrument by a practised hand. She had crossed the room, and stood close beside him; her hands were clasped together, her small head was held erect. Her eyes were darkened by anger. He looked up surprised, and slightly disturbed. He felt some annoyance at an interruption so unaccustomed. The seclusion of his library

was broken in upon in a manner which was
a bad omen for its future security.

'Pray tell me what has annoyed you?'
he said, rather coldly.

'I cannot stay here,' repeated Virginia,
quickly, but still with the distinctness
which indicates a certain amount of self-
control. 'I came here willingly. I thought
it was kind of Mrs. Stansfield to offer me a
home, and I was grateful.'

'And how has that undeserved claim
upon your gratitude been forfeited?'

But she did not heed his question.

'I know,' she continued, 'I had no
right to complain. No one was unkind to
me. I could not say that my presence
was either welcome or unwelcome. Till
this afternoon, I was content to remain
here.'

'And this afternoon?' he questioned,
with a slight access of curiosity.

'This afternoon a proposal was made to
me which was an insult,' cried Virginia;

and suddenly like a fire that will not be suppressed the colour rose and burnt in her cheeks. 'Hartley has before now thrust unwelcome attentions upon me. I excused him because he knew no better, and it was not altogether his fault ; his mother pressed him on. But now,' drawing her breath quickly—'Now that he takes advantage of my position here not only to entreat but to urge and almost command me to give him a promise of marriage; when he plainly asserts that he will take no refusal, and that upon every opportunity either with or against my will he will repeat his offer ; it becomes nothing less than a persecution to which I will not submit.'

Mr. Stansfield remained silent for a moment. Perhaps his chief feeling was one of astonishment that it should be in that room that her indignation should have found a voice; but his astonishment was not unmixed with other more complex feelings.

'You are certainly not bound to submit to it,' he said, after that momentary pause; 'but is it not,' and he glanced at her for an instant—'Is it not rather hard to stigmatize pertinacity so natural as an insult.'

'No, it is not,' answered Virginia, decidedly. 'The wording, the manner of his proposal left no doubt upon that point:' and at the recollection tears of shame and mortification rushed to her eyes. 'I was alone in the conservatory or he would not have dared to say what he did. You think that I need not be so angry, but—I wish that you had been there.'

'I cannot echo that wish,' cried Norton, only restrained by the sight of her tears from unseemly laughter. 'It would have been a dangerous position to have taken up to very little purpose, since I feel assured you were well able to defend yourself.'

'It ought not to have been necessary,' cried Virginia, with a flash of spirit.

'I should have needed no defence; my position, alone and friendless, should have been sufficient. I used to trust everyone; now Hartley has not only taught me to distrust himself but others also; he has spoilt it all.'

She sat down and leaned her head upon her hands, and under their shelter the tears fell upon the scattered papers on his writing-table. Norton was very much discomfited. He already felt himself to be in an anomalous position. He had not been disposed to regard Hartley's boyish misdemeanours in any very serious light; it was perfectly natural that he should make love to his pretty cousin, he would have been surprised if he had not done so, especially when encouraged by his mother; and at first it had appeared to him that Virginia's indignation was uncalled for. He felt no apprehensions upon her account; as he had said, she was able to defend herself; but if her defence were to cost her such bitter tears, and to be undertaken at the price of such a cruel disillusionment, it became a very different matter, and he could not maintain his indifference.

'Hartley has been very wrong,' he began, ' but why should you take it so much to heart? It was to have been expected; he has behaved badly, but . . .'

'But you are not really angry with him,' cried Virginia, raising her wet eyes to him in quick reproach. 'I thought you at least would take my part. You do not seem to understand that I have a right to be angry.'

'You have every right, only that he is not worth your anger,' he answered. 'Let us talk of this reasonably. You seem to think that in these matters a woman has unlimited power. If it were so, remember that there would be no unrequited attachments, no rejected love. This world,' smiling, 'would be a duller but undoubtedly a happier place.'

'But I do not know what you mean to imply.'

'Merely that you cannot forbid Hartley to love you with any reasonable chance of being obeyed,' answered Norton, calmly.

'It is not the least necessary. He,' with a little scorn, 'is in no danger. Mrs. Stansfield, for some reasons of her own, wishes him to marry me. He is simply carrying out her instructions.'

The shrewdness of her observation took Mr. Stansfield by surprise. He had not imagined that a young girl would have been so clear-sighted, and he was inclined to believe that she was right.

'Yet this supposition is hardly corroborated by his conduct to-day,' he observed aloud.

'I do not think that it contradicts it. He has tried other methods and they have none of them succeeded. He at last adopted another tone upon principle.'

'And met with like ill success?'

She nodded her head, but did not speak. Now that the first flush of indignation was over she looked somewhat depressed, and sat still, passing a ribbon which held some papers together slowly through her fingers.

'I am afraid of being presumptuous,' he said, after a minute or two, 'and you are evidently severe upon presumption. At the same time I feel that I could better repay your confidence if you would extend it so far as to let me know the exact position in which you stand towards Hartley. He has offended you, but yet until now you were good friends.'

'We were never *friends;*' and she laid an emphasis on the word. 'But he was the first to give me a welcome when I came here, and it is true I liked him; but he knew that I had no one here to take my part, and he took advantage of it. It was not fair,' with returning anger. 'I shall never like him again.'

'It is not for me to appeal against that

sentence,' he answered, ' but you said just now that he knew you had no one to take your part. I trust that you will not say that any longer, and, if we can persuade him to the contrary, may I not hope that you will recall your determination to leave Stansfield ?'

' But it would never do for me to be a cause of dissension in the family,' said Virginia, shaking her head. ' If you take my part, Mrs. Stansfield will be very angry.'

' That prospect does not alarm me.'

' And Hartley will quarrel with you.'

' I never quarrel.'

' But if you threaten him . . .'

' I never threaten—I strike.'

' Do not strike anyone upon my account,' cried Virginia, glancing at him with some trepidation. ' Only Hartley must never speak to me again as he did this afternoon. If I remain, it must be upon that understanding.'

' You appealed to me just now as

master of the house. The designation may not be absolutely correct, but at least my authority extends far enough to protect you from further annoyance. Will you give me leave to exercise it? If it were not so,' and now he spoke gravely enough, ' you should leave us, if you desired it, to-night.'

Virginia remained silent. In the bewilderment of her novel experiences her self-confidence had for the moment deserted her. The curtains were still withdrawn, though the dusk had gathered thickly outside and the candles were already lighted. Mr. Stansfield sat with his back to them, and his sombre eyes looked out from among the shadows. As Virginia turned from them uneasily, it seemed to her that a form passed across the darkened square of the window, and there was a sound as of stealthy footsteps upon the gravel.

'There is some one outside,' she cried, starting.

' Do not alarm yourself,' he said, coolly.
'In all probability it is no one more for-
midable than Mr. Marshall, who not infrequently pays me these uncalled-for
attentions. He gives himself a great deal
of trouble to very little purpose.'

Nevertheless, he stepped to the window
and drew down the blind before replacing
some papers in his despatch-box.

' And I have been hindering you all this
time.' And Virginia looked a little re-
morseful.

'Terribly,' he answered, with a smile ;
but he could not help giving a somewhat
dismayed glance at his disordered papers.
She had been resting her arm upon the
table, and at once seized the meaning of
his involuntary look.

' It is my fault, Mr. Stansfield. I am
sorry.'

But as she spoke the ribbon with which
she had been playing slipped in her fin-

gers, and the documents which it fastened were scattered upon the floor.

'How unlucky I am!' cried Virginia, going down upon her knees to pick them up.

'Pray do not give yourself that trouble,' he said, somewhat stiffly; 'I shall get them into order again presently.'

'I really think I ought to stay and help you,' she answered, rising, with her hands full of papers. 'I have done you a great deal of mischief.'

'But quite involuntarily.'

'Certainly it would be bad policy in a land of strangers,' sighing, 'to quarrel with one's only friend.'

'But are you quite sure that you will not quarrel with me?'

'Yes, I am sure of it. I would, on the contrary, do you a kindness if I could.'

'Yet I have done nothing to deserve it.'

'Do not say that; you have befriended

me more than once. Have you forgotten,' smiling, 'my supper in the library?'

'Whereby you escaped a most salutary lesson. You took the weaker side, and yet you did not suffer for it. It was a pity; you may be tempted to do it again.'

'I do not see why you should laugh at me.' She looked a little hurt as she walked towards the door. 'It was only right that I should take Mademoiselle Joseph's part. She could not defend herself.'

'Right,' he echoed, with rather a melancholy smile. 'I am not laughing at you, I assure you. No doubt many of us begin life as if it were a pilgrim's progress, and I am afraid you will consider me an untrustworthy guide upon the way; still just now I should like you to follow my guidance.'

'Where will it lead me?' asked Virginia, hesitating. He had wounded her pride, and yet she was unwilling to leave him; she had no one else to whom to go.

'It will lead you to remain—for the present, at least—at Stansfield,' he answered, with decision. 'I am truly sorry that anything disagreeable should be connected with your visit; but there shall be no repetition of it. I will speak to Hartley, and he shall not annoy you again.'

His manner was a little distant, but not wanting in kindness, yet for the first time Virginia looked a little abashed. Possibly she felt that upon the impulse of the moment she had shown him a confidence which was at once uncalled-for and undesired.

'But I do not know what I ought to do,' she said, trembling, once more upon the verge of tears.

'Then will you let me judge for you? You said just now that you were friendless and alone here.'

'It is true. I have only Mademoiselle Joseph.'

'Is that all?' he asked. She looked at him inquiringly, but made no answer. 'Is that all?' he repeated. 'When you number up your friends, will you not count me amongst them?'

'Surely,' she answered, with a friendly smile. Mortification and anger had melted under the kindness of the look which he bent upon her, like snow in the sunshine. 'Then, if you wish it, I will remain.' She paused, with her hand upon the door, and added, with the mixture of childlike simplicity and fearlessness which distinguished her manner, 'You have been very kind. I had no one else to whom to appeal.'

'You were perfectly right,' he answered, a little stiffly, perhaps feeling the incongruity of his position as a young girl's adviser, as he opened the door to let her pass.

CHAPTER XI.

IT was nearly dark, and a drizzling rain was falling thick as mist, persistent and penetrating. At the corner of a footpath which led from the front gate to the back-door of the house Virginia was standing, though the evergreens above her head were dripping with moisture, and the gravel beneath her feet was soaked and yielding. She was evidently waiting for something or somebody; for every now and then she moved restlessly, and put out her head from under the poor shelter which she had chosen, straining her eyes through the darkness to see if anyone approached. Already many times before in the chill winds she had stolen out to keep her watch, so that she might, if possible, snatch the comfort for which she yearned so eagerly but a few minutes sooner; only to have her hopes more quickly dashed, and to learn that her watch had been kept in vain. And yet, not altogether in vain; since at least Mademoiselle Joseph need not see the dumb disappointment in her face; since at least she need not fear her Aunt Charlotte's cheerful comment as she sorted the letters: 'No letter for you to-night, Virginia.'

And it was many weeks since Virginia had had a letter. Sometimes a great dread settled like a black cloud upon her spirits; more often a restless fever of anxiety burnt within her—and yet she never spoke of it, not even now to Mademoiselle Joseph. With all her frankness, there was a fund of reserve in her nature, an element of courage which forbade her to cry aloud in her trouble. Dexter, the postman, knew her well. He was prepared for the hand half outstretched to him through the darkness, and the whispered question: 'Is there one for me, Dexter?' And he would have given a good deal to have been able to return an answer in the affirmative.

He was surely later than usual this evening. Virginia drew out her watch in the vain endeavour to discover the position of the hands on its small disk. At the same instant she heard steps approaching, but it was not the steady, plodding tread of the messenger whom she was awaiting; these were light, half-running footsteps, accompanied by a boy's high whistle, and the next moment, before she had time to step out of his way, Jack stumbled against her.

'Don't be frightened, my dear,' he ejaculated; 'I won't tell of you. But it is too wet a night for you to expect your sweetheart.' Then, suddenly becoming aware of the tall, slight figure whom he was addressing : 'Good gracious, Virginia, is it you?   I thought it was Polly, the kitchen-maid.'

'You certainly have a remarkable talent for appearing when you are least wanted,' answered Virginia, a little crossly.   'I thought that you were upstairs in the school-room.'

'And I imagined you safe in the drawing-room, which is a much more proper place for a young woman than a wet shrubbery on a December evening.   I cannot say that I approve of this; it is like a flower in your bonnet—one never knows what it may lead to.   I don't think it is right, I really don't.   Pray, let me hear what you have to say for yourself.'

'Don't be ridiculous,' cried Virginia, giving him a little shake.   'I came,' faltering a little, 'to meet the postman.'

'Oh, a very plausible story.   When I return to school and write you love-letters, let me beg that you will receive them openly before the family. Anything underhand absolutely repels me.'

'Listen, there is some one coming,' whispered Virginia, paying no attention to his last remark. 'Be quiet; I do not wish to be seen.'

'You are quite right, for it is a compromising situation, and it is not the postman.' He had edged himself close up to her and was peering out under the shadow of the laurel-bushes. 'By all that is wonderful,' as the steps and subdued voices drew near, 'by all that is wonderful it is Hartley, and Hartley hates water like a new-fledged chicken.'

Virginia laid a small wet hand upon his mouth. She had no wish to meet Hartley.

'He is up to mischief,' continued the boy, gently pushing her hand aside and speaking in low, hoarse tones. Jack's voice was cracking and he was pleased to affect the bass notes of a maturer age as being most within his compass, though they were diversified against his will by a high and unmusical treble. 'He would not be out on this wet evening for any good. Oh, I know his ways! Just put your head down a little, Virginia, and you will see him coming up the approach. I am sure he has been up to some mischief, for Marshall is with him. Oh, if I had but my air-gun, or even my best pea-shooter.'

By this time, however, the two upon whom he had these amiable designs were close upon them, and even Jack saw the necessity of silence if he would not be discovered. Virginia would willingly have beaten a retreat, but for the moment she was hemmed in. She had gathered up her skirts in one hand prepared for instant flight if they should advance upon her, but as it happened, walking close together, and conversing in low tones, they turned into a side-path leading in another direction.

'Do they not look like conspirators?' asked Jack, raising himself from a crouching position to brush the wet mould from his trousers. 'And if they have a plot, depend upon it, it is against Norton. I wish I could find it out. Though why should I care about a cold-blooded ungrateful half-brother who thinks it a pity that I was born?'

'Yet you would like to do him a kindness! You really must be a good boy, after all.'

'I am—awfully good. I am an avenging angel; the wicked shall not go unpunished if I can help it. I know Marshall's nasty spiteful ways of old. It would be a sacred duty to " confound their politics, frustrate their knavish tricks." Have you never learnt to sing " God Save the Queen," Virginia?'

'I do not see that they can do Mr. Stansfield any harm,' she answered, as she emerged from the shrubbery on to the gravel walk. 'I feel rather like a conspirator myself. It is very cold. There can be no post to-night,' sighing, 'I shall go in.'

The drawing-room looked warm and pleasant after the chill dampness outside, when Virginia returned to it. The curtains were drawn across the windows. Emmeline sat at her embroidery frame, and Mr. Stansfield stood upon the rug with a newspaper in his hands. His step-mother was busied at the tea-table. She liked these small domestic duties. She wrote her own notes, made her own tea, and felt it rather a grievance that she was no longer able to carve at her own dinner-table.

Virginia drew a chair up to the fire and opened a book; but, though it lay upon her knees and her eyes were fixed upon it, her thoughts were far away. She saw a long string of camels crossing a desert, and in the distance a glare as of fire in the sky, and a sick man lying alone within his tent. She started when her aunt's voice struck upon her ears, and the question had to be repeated before she was roused from her abstraction.

'What have you been doing with yourself on this miserable afternoon, Virginia?'

'I?' cried the girl, starting. 'I have been upstairs with Mademoiselle Joseph.'

'You were quite right to stay indoors. It was not a fit day for anyone to be out,' answered Mrs. Stansfield, pouring exactly the right quantity of tea into her thin, china cups.

Virginia looked up for an instant and met Mr. Stansfield's eyes bent upon her with a kind of amused inquiry; following the direction of his glance, she perceived its cause. She had laid aside her cloak and hat in the hall, but the edges of her dress were heavy with rain, and one or two dead leaves lay in its folds which had not escaped his keen observation. She coloured, and hastily pushed them out of sight.

'I thought that you had no secrets,' he said, in a low voice, as he brought her a cup of tea.

'The post is later and later every day,' observed Mrs. Stansfield, as, her duties at the tea-table being ended, she drew forward an easy-chair and took up her knitting.

'It came in, however, half-an-hour ago, mamma,' said Emmeline. 'For they brought in the evening paper.'

'Ah, I wanted to see that. There should be some news by this time, I think . . .'

She broke off in the middle of her sentence as Norton, pushing against a little table near him, put down a cup and saucer. In the midst of her lamentations over the carpet and the ringing of the bell for the housemaid, Mr. Stansfield, muttering a hasty apology, escaped from the room; but he had not got further than

the hall when Virginia's voice arrested
him.

'You have the evening paper, Mr. Stansfield, and I know that there is some news
from—Egypt.'

'It is all conjecture,' he answered, with
a calmness which helped to quiet her fluttering pulses. 'If it were not so, I should
not have desired to keep it from you.'
And, without any further hesitation, he
lighted one of the candles upon the hall
chimney-piece by which they stood, and,
handing her the paper which he held, he
pointed out the paragraph.

'They are not even certain of the regi-
ment, you see,' he continued, after a pause,
in which she had had time to scan the few
lines which spoke of an engagement in
which the English losses had been heavy.
'I think myself that the probabilities are
in favour of Colonel Tennant's safety.
Will you not try to believe it?'

'It is so long since I have had a letter,'

she sighed, too much oppressed by fear to give way to tears.

'I know it,' he answered, kindly. 'Do you imagine I have not watched you come in late with pale cheeks to breakfast; have I not seen your light burning long after you should have been peacefully asleep. Are not the post-hours the moments for which you live throughout the day.'

'You knew it!' she exclaimed, astounded at the closeness of his observation. What other person in the house had taken the trouble to wonder if she were glad or sorrowful, anxious or at rest!

'Did you think yourself so experienced a dissembler?' he answered, with a smile. 'I knew it, and I was sorry for it. It is not wise to anticipate troubles. Have our woods and gardens lost their charm for you? You said at first they were attractive even in their wintry dress; but now you hardly go outside the house, or only at the most untimely moments, as, for example,' with a keen glance at her, 'this evening. Consider weeks may elapse before you receive any certain tidings, and you must take courage.'

'I used not to be afraid,' she answered, drawing a little closer to him, as if glad of the encouragement of his words. 'But now I cannot help it. I fear—the worst; and at night in the darkness,' shivering even in the warmth of the great hall-fire, 'I see dead faces, and the smoke and flash of battles, and I cannot sleep, and when I sleep I dream.'

'That is because you are weak and nervous,' he said, with decision, though there was some anxiety in his dark eyes. 'You should walk out more, and when it is wet read a novel, instead of sitting unoccupied. You had a book upon your knees the other night, and not once during the whole evening did you turn a page. If you dream when you are awake, it is no wonder that you should dream at night.

And I am afraid,' after a pause, 'that here you have no companion.'

'Emmeline is so much older and wiser,' answered the girl, evasively. 'And Hartley has rather avoided me since—since I spoke to you. But it is not that, and after all—' with a smile as bright and fleeting as sunshine after rain—'after all, I have always Jack.'

'Jack!' he echoed, with unaffected surprise.

'Yes, he is a bad boy, but I like him. He is a very bad boy to other people, but he is generally good to me, and I like him,' cried Virginia, as she turned and ran up the stairs to dress for dinner.

'Well, there is certainly no accounting for tastes,' muttered Norton to himself.

CHAPTER XII.

VIRGINIA thought of the counsel Mr. Stansfield had given her when she went to her room that evening, and remembered his words only to discover how impossible it was to put them into practice. More persistently than before her mind had reverted to Egypt, and upon another battlefield hopes and fears strove together in an unavailing struggle. She could make no attempt to compose herself to slumber. A feverish anxiety burnt like a consuming fire in her heart.

'Oh, if I could but know,' she said, restlessly, to herself, as she sat on a low chair by her bed-room fire.

It was a tranquil night; no wind stirred in the trees, and within the house there reigned that intense stillness which so often becomes oppressive to the solitary watcher. It was not yet twelve o'clock, but Mrs. Stansfield and Emmeline had retired to rest an hour ago. Mr. Stansfield was the only member of that household who kept any solitary vigils, and he was dining out at a distant neighbour's. She had heard him tell his step-mother that he should necessarily be late, and should let himself in with his latchkey. No sound broke the silence but the flicker of the fire and the steady ticking of the clock in the passage below.

She rose to her feet, and, walking to the window, drew aside the curtain and looked out. The lawns lay white in the starlight, the quiet woods fringed the horizon. The world was wrapped in soft, unbroken sleep, and within the house too all was still as ever; yet even as she gazed a glimmer of light, first faint and then brighter, shone out from a downstairs window upon the path below. Virginia observed it at first indifferently, and then a sudden thought struck her. Her window was immediately above the hall-door; it would have been hardly possible for Mr. Stansfield to have entered by that way without her being aware of it. She must surely in the stillness of the night have heard him open that heavy door and put up the chain, and yet this light most certainly came from the library. Who but himself could be there in Mr. Stansfield's own private apartments at this hour. She blew out her candle and set herself to watch, kneeling upon the floor with her arms on the window-sill. Her heart beat a little quickly with excitement. It was not the least likely that an ordinary burglar would have selected that quarter of the house for his operations. There was nothing of value except the heavy old furniture and a few pictures, but it was in that room that Mr. Stansfield kept all his private papers, and it was just possible that some one might be ransacking them in his absence.

Virginia shivered a little but was pleasurably excited. She had already half-forgotten her more pressing anxieties in the thought of some danger to the absent master of the house; not for the world would she have left her post. He should have at least one defender.

As a clock struck the hour, listening intently, she detected stealthy movements in the lower part of the house, as if some one were pushing about the furniture; then the light inside was suddenly extinguished, and the next instant the figure of a man emerged from a side door and took a few cautious steps in the direction of the shrubberies. It was not possible to discern his features, but it was light enough for Virginia to recognise the thin figure and peculiar gait of her aunt's factotum, Mr. Marshall.

'Jack was right,' she said to herself. 'He is a conspirator, and Mr. Stansfield's enemy. But he shall not escape unobserved.'

Too indignant to be timid, she took up her candle and passed with quick, light footsteps along the matted corridor and down the broad staircase. She crossed the darkened hall, on whose hearth a few logs yet redly smouldered, and pushing aside the heavy curtain entered the library. It was unoccupied. For the first time Virginia, as she stood looking around her, felt a movement of fear. Her candle made but a feeble spot of light in the darkness; the corners of the room remained in shadow, the statue glimmered white in a recess, and the outlines of the furniture looked ghostly and unfamiliar. She started at the sound of a distant door and turned to escape to the security of her own room;

but as she drew aside the portière she paused irresolute. Another light was advancing towards her across the hall, and Mr. Stansfield, who carried it, was looking about him in evident perplexity. But Virginia, whose courage had returned to her, had no longer any desire to escape.

'Mr. Stansfield,' she cried, in a low voice. 'Come here.'

He turned at her call, and his eyes lighted upon her with unconcealed astonishment.

'I thought I saw a light down this passage, and was nerving myself for the worst, he said, smiling, but somewhat uneasily. 'And instead of a burglar I find you.'

'But some one was here before me. I am sure of it,' cried Virginia, quickly. 'I saw the light from my window. That is the reason that I came down. It was Marshall; I am certain of it. I saw him as he walked away.'

'Marshall!' he echoed, with displeased surprise.

He passed his eye quickly over the undisturbed bookshelves, the papers on the table, the dispatch-box in its usual place and then he regarded Virginia herself again with a little anxiety.

'You sit up too late and get nervous,' he said, kindly. 'I am very sorry that you should have had an alarm, but the light which you saw was probably carried by one of the gardeners going to attend to the hothouses, or the policeman making his rounds.'

'Then I hope he may come across Mr. Marshall, for it was Marshall I saw,' answered Virginia, positively.

He made no reply, but still looked sceptical.

'I wish I could find some traces of his presence to convince you,' cried Virginia, looking round; then as if she had detected something she moved forward hastily and laid her hand upon the shutter; it was not bolted. As she pushed it aside the window itself flew open; it was not fastened.

'Was not this window shut up for the night?' asked Virginia. Then, in a lower voice: 'He stepped out from it. Listen, I almost think I can hear some one outside at this moment.'

'Then let us shut them out,' he said, hastily; and drawing her back into the room he bolted the window and put up the bar of the shutter. Virginia looked surprised.

'Are you afraid?' she asked.

'I am. And you?'

'I am afraid sometimes,' she answered, 'but not of robbers, certainly not of Mr. Marshall. I should like him to be found out. He must be a bad man.'

'Though I can lay no claim to your courage, I think you had better leave him to me,' answered Norton, looking a good deal discomposed. 'It is very late, and you must be tired. Pray do not let this little adventure disturb your rest.'

'I shall not be likely to dream of Mr. Marshall,' answered Virginia, a little disdainfully.

'And stay, one moment,' said Norton. She turned and looked back at him. 'Do not mention this to Mrs. Stansfield or Emmeline. It would alarm them to no purpose. I will take measures to ensure the security of the house in future.'

But it was not for the security of the house that he was fearing as he stood by the empty hearth after she had left him. 'Could he have seen her?' he asked himself, anxiously. 'He is powerless against me, but, if he has seen her, how easily may his vile tongue do her an injury.' He took out his keys and opened his desk; the key moved a little stiffly in the ward; he fancied that the lock might have been tampered with, but could not be certain. Yet even as he turned over his papers his mind reverted to Virginia. She had acted upon a kind and generous impulse and was heedless of the consequences, yet she had undoubtedly run a risk for his sake. He hardly knew whether the reflection pleased or annoyed him, but he was roused out of his ordinary composure. He did not deceive himself as to Virginia's motives. She had acted out of pure kindliness of spirit, she would have done the same for anyone who happened to have befriended her; he thought of her running down without a moment's hesitation to face an unknown enemy on her friend's behalf. 'Poor child, she has a kind heart,' he said to himself, with a smile and a sigh.

Mr. Marshall's curiosity did not disturb him much. The papers which he sought were in safe keeping at the lawyer's. Perhaps past experience had made Mr. Stansfield cautious, and he was not afraid of being outwitted. Nevertheless, it was disheartening to feel that he was, as it were, an alien within his own gates. No one but this girl, herself a stranger, would care if he went out from them never to return. He thought of his unloved boyhood, of the dull sense of injury under repeated injustice which had embittered his most natural affections. There had been nothing left for him to love but the familiar surroundings : the old house, the walled garden, the woods and pastures to which his mind clung with the unreasoning tenacity of a son of the soil. He never spoke of Stansfield, yet he had borne his step-mother's ceaseless persecutions, and all the uncongenial adjuncts of his life there, rather than leave it, and borne them too with severe, though somewhat sullen self-control. It had not been so difficult of late, not so hard since one face at least brightened at his approach, and one hand was stretched out to him in warm and friendly greeting. He felt that she liked him ; and he was grateful to her for it. She had trusted him; he wished that it might be in his power to make her some return.

In the meantime Virginia, passing quickly along the upstairs corridor, had been startled by a hoarse whisper through a half-opened door.

'Is the house on fire? Never mind if it is. It will be all right. I always keep the garden syringe under my bed. I'll have it out ready in a minute.'

'Do not be so silly,' answered Virginia, laughing a little under her breath. 'It is nothing of the sort. It was only that I saw a light and thought . . .'

'Robbers!' ejaculated Master Jack, in jubilant *crescendo*. 'My word, how lucky! Why didn't you call me before. I know where Norton keeps his pistols. Get out of my way, Virginia, and when you hear the first shot pull the alarm bell in the servants' passage; if only that stalking image of a policeman is anywhere about won't he

run to report himself at head-quarters when
he hears it.'

'Jack, if you do not be quiet and go
back to bed directly, I will never forgive
you,' cried Virginia. 'There are no
robbers, no chance of fire, nor anything
at all interesting. I shall be dreadfully
angry if you wake the house, but I will
make an honourable compact with you if
you will be quiet now: I will tell you all
that has happened in the morning. I shall
not tell anyone else.'

Jack hesitated and wavered, but the
bribe appealed both to his curiosity and
his pride. In five minutes he was asleep
again, whilst Virginia too lay down to rest,
and, diverted from the thought of her own
troubles, slept more soundly than she had
done for weeks.

She awoke refreshed, and for the moment
free from that dull half-conscious sense of
sorrow which had so often of late weighed

down her spirits. It was a cheerless morning, and through the uncurtained windows she could see the low mist which hung over the park; but she opened her eyes upon it with a smile, clasped her hands behind her head upon the pillow, thought of Mr. Stansfield's surprise and of Jack's prompt and warlike preparations, and laughed outright.

'Don't forget your promise,' cried Jack, drawing her aside as soon as breakfast was over. 'You know, Virginia, I am naturally unsuspicious, and I did not think of it at the moment, but what were you doing out of your bed at that time of night? If the house was not on fire, and if there were no robbers about, why where you not asleep and dreaming? I am really afraid that, if it were not for me, you would be getting yourself into some scrape.'

'Do try to be serious for once.' Virginia pulled him down into one of the dining-room window-seats beside her. The rest of the party had already left the room and they were alone. ' Be serious for a moment, for really this is no laughing matter. You remember seeing your brother and Marshall talking together, you said that they looked like conspirators; well, I believe that you were right. Marshall, at any rate, would get the better of Mr. Stansfield, if he could. I am sure of it. I saw him as plainly as possible come creeping out of the library window last night. I ran downstairs, and met Mr. Stansfield in the hall. He would not believe me at first; but he was obliged to acknowledge that the shutter was unfastened and the window open.'

'And you never called me. You let me miss it all. Well! I did not think that you would have done it.'

He turned from her in real vexation, and began drumming a tune upon the window-pane with his fingers.

'I had no time to think of you, nor of

anything else,' answered Virginia, sooth-
ingly. 'If I had stopped to think, I should
have been too much frightened to go down
at all.'

'What! frightened of Marshall?'

'No, not of Marshall, but . . . of the
dark passages and empty rooms. It was
all so still, and I was all alone.'

'That was your own fault. Still, I believe you are sorry now; so we will say no
more about it. Only I would wish you to
remember, Virginia, that repentance cannot undo the past. But let us consider.
Cannot we lay some trap to induce Marshall to come back again? If I could only
catch him . . . .'

'What mischief are you two concocting?'
asked Mr. Stansfield, pausing on the gravel
path outside the window.

A gleam of sunshine, breaking through
the mist, rested upon the girl's smooth
dark head and the boy's fair one bent close
together. Jack looked up at him a little

sulkily, but Virginia smiled, and pushed the window open.

'We are concocting an alliance offensive and defensive on your behalf, Mr. Stans-field.'

'That is very kind of you,' he answered; 'but where is the enemy?'

'Ah! that is just the question,' cried Jack. 'Now, if Virginia had only called me up—as she ought to have done—last night, I can promise you that he should not have got off.'

'You mean Marshall,' observed Mr. Stans-field, very composedly, knocking the ashes off the end of his cigar. 'He is hardly a worthy subject for your valour. If it were worth while, he should be dismissed to-morrow; but I can give him a hint which will keep him upon his good behaviour for the future.'

'But why should you allow him to remain?' asked Virginia.

'It pleases Mrs. Stansfield that he should

do so,' he answered, a little coldly. 'He is harmless enough, but he is a monomaniac. He has some vision of trust deeds, or documents concerning the estate, which, if they came into his hands, would make his fortune. He imagines that I secrete them in the library. A denial would only confirm him in his opinion; besides, I am not inclined to take Mr. Marshall into my confidence.'

'Nor anyone else,' muttered Jack, turning his back upon his half-brother.

'Nor anyone else,' repeated Norton, smiling.

The boy shook himself, and walked off, whistling rather defiantly, and slammed the door behind him.

'Now, there I think you are wrong,' cried Virginia. 'What would this world be without some one whom you can trust, without a friend—some one whom you believe in, and who believes in you? Would it not be too dismal a place to live in?'

'But, unfortunately, we are not allowed any choice in the matter.'

He looked down, a little amused at her eagerness.

'Well, I do not agree with you,' she said, a little impatiently. 'I am glad to be alive, very glad.'

'And, believe me,' and he bent his earnest gaze upon her flushed, upturned face—'Believe me, I share in your gladness. The world is a better place since you are in it.'

'I am very glad that you think so. It is kind of you to say it.'

She looked frankly delighted. She had had so very few words of praise since she came to Stansfield, and she had no idea of concealing her natural satisfaction. She remembered how Hartley had once said, 'Even Norton is changed since you came here.' Was it possible that he was right? Had she, could she have, any sort of power over Mr. Stansfield?

'Why are you not happy?' she asked, abruptly.

'Why!' he echoed, with a curious smile. 'Is anyone?'

'I was, I was perfectly happy; I shall be so again when papa comes home. Do you not believe it?'

'Believe in what—in happiness?' He spoke reluctantly—no, he did not believe in it, yet he hesitated to cast a shadow upon her confidence or shake the faith vouchsafed to so few.

'You need not be afraid to speak,' said Virginia, with her usual quickness divining his unspoken thought. 'I shall not mind; what you say will make no difference to me.'

'Yet I thought that you professed some respect for my judgment.'

'But this is a subject upon which I am afraid you cannot speak from experience, and I wonder why?' asked Virginia, looking thoughtful. 'You are an eldest son, and people in England think a great deal of that, do they not? You have plenty of money and a beautiful place to live in. You are fond of reading, and you have leisure for study. You are never ill, and . . .'

'Oh, if you only knew how low-spirited you make me by this catalogue of my advantages,' interrupted Norton, looking slightly irritated. 'Could you not for once look at the other side of the picture.'

'I never look at more than one side of anything;' and she laughed. 'You may have another side to your character, but it does not matter to me.'

'That bespeaks indifference, I am afraid.'

'No, only when I hear . . . when Mrs. Stansfield and Emmeline for instance, when . . .' She broke off, hesitating, and bent down her head, blushing in sudden confusion.

'Pray go on. You need not be afraid.

I think I can bear to hear even what
Mrs. Stansfield and Emmeline say of
me.'

'It is only that it seems unkind even to
repeat it,' she said, softly.   'But when
they say that you are gloomy and harsh-
tempered and selfish I am very angry,
though I suppose that you . . .'

'Yes, that I?'

'That you are not the same to them as
to me.'

'And you are perfectly right in that
conjecture, though you advance it so
timidly,' he said, with the light of laughter
in his eyes. 'Thank Heaven, you are
neither my step-mother nor my half-sister.
Come, you have given me all the darker
shades of the picture—gloomy, harsh-tem-
pered, and selfish; it is not exactly a pleasant sketch; can you not see some lights
amongst the shadows?'

He had thrown away his cigar, and

leaned against the wall with his hand upon the window-sill.

'Look and see,' he demanded, half in jest and half in earnest, 'are there not some lights amidst the shadows?'

Virginia looked up slowly and hesitatingly. She seemed a little shy, and her eyes rested upon the slight yet muscular hand upon the window frame, and upon the sleeve of his shooting-jacket, before she lifted them to his face.

'You have been very kind to me,' she said, gravely. 'I think you are melancholy sometimes but you have a good heart, I have seen it, you always help the weak. I should not like to stay at Stansfield unless you were here. I know that you . . .'

'Virginia, what can you be thinking of?' asked a voice in the dining-room behind. 'What a terrible draught on this raw morning. You will be certain to catch cold.'

'There was no draught until you opened the door,' answered Virginia, coolly, moving, however, to shut the sash. 'I did not feel cold.'

'But it was very imprudent, and, if Hartley has not yet gone, he will be late.'

'I was not talking to Hartley,' answered Virginia, a little haughtily. 'It was Mr. Stansfield.'

She slipped from the window-seat, stopped for an instant to pick up a book which had fallen on to the floor, and left the room.

As Norton was walking across the fields on his way to a distant farm, he smiled a little to himself. A ray of sunlight had penetrated into his darkened and solitary life. Some one at least had an absolute, unfounded, unreasonable trust in him; all the more prized on account of its unreasonableness. The frank liking this young girl had shown him was something altogether new and unexpected. Stansfield was a different place to him since she had said, 'I should not like to stay at Stansfield if you were not there.'

CHAPTER XIII.

'I FEEL rather forlorn,' said Virginia. She was standing under the portico, and on the steps behind her Mr. Stansfield was, with some difficulty, lighting his cigar. It was a stormy day early in February; the north wind swept the leaves along the ground, and rustled the creepers above his head.

'Forlorn! how is that?' he enquired, as he descended the steps.

During the last month, he and Virginia had made some advances in intimacy. She had not infrequently sought his advice. She had read books of his selection, and by dint of unremitting occupation had striven to keep anxiety at bay. If her interest in what went on around her was less keen, if her step was less light, and her smile less ready, none of her relations were likely to disturb themselves about it. She had indeed had the comfort of a few hurried lines from Colonel Tennant, but it seemed to her that the silence was all the more oppressive after that one letter.

'Yes, I feel very forlorn to-day,' she repeated, twisting a spray of ivy in her fingers.

'Yet you will not tell me why.'

'Because I hardly know the reason. I think I have an accumulation of reasons. This is such a depressing sunless morning, and I could not sleep last night, my head aches, and you are going away to-day.'

'That is the last, and I fear the least of your troubles.'

'By no means. I shall miss you very often. I am sorry that you are going, very sorry.'

Her evident sincerity was at once
flattering and disappointing, and so, perhaps, Mr. Stansfield thought, for a rather
dubious expression crossed his face, and he
remained silent.

'And you are going in a few minutes,
are you not?' she continued; 'when will you
return?'

'It is easier to answer your first question
than your second. I cannot exactly tell
when I may return; but I have still half-
an-hour to spare, shall we see if we can
find any shelter in the garden?'

'For your cigar?' and she laughed with
a touch of her old light-heartedness; but
her gaiety was transitory, and she was
grave enough as they walked together
through the leafless shrubberies. The
wide wintry landscape lay before them;
swept by the strong wind, it was as grey
and desolate as the heavens above.

'Is it not the very day for a parting?'
asked Virginia, and then stopped suddenly,

her speech arrested by the poignant memory of 'another parting hour; she saw again the storm-tossed waters of the Channel, and a confused sound of wind and waves was in her ears. 'I wish that the world were not so wide,' she cried, sighing.

'An unwise wish, since we might not then find it so easy to get away from un-desired companions. From Mrs. Stans-field, for example.' Then, after an instant's pause: 'I should not have left Stansfield if Hartley had been at home.'

'But I thought that you were going on urgent business?'

'Yet there might have been a cause strong enough to demand its postpone-ment.'

'Would you have remained upon my account?' cried Virginia, looking pleased and surprised.

'Why should you doubt it?'

'I did not think that anyone cared . . .' she stopped and looked down at the ground, not in the least embarrassed, but a little perplexed.

'Do not have such thoughts any longer,' he said, kindly. 'It is quite true that I would upon no account have left you here with Hartley. I may be wrong, but I do not trust him. It would have been far better if he had had any pride or vanity upon which your rejection would have inflicted an irreparable wound. He has neither the one nor the other, and he will find it only too easy to forgive you.'

'But I shall not find it easy to forgive him,' cried Virginia, indignantly. 'It is not only that he does not care for me for my own sake, but he knows that I know it, and yet he still thought himself at liberty, just to save appearances, to profess an affection which he did not feel and imagined that I should be ready to believe, or rather to pretend to believe in it.'

'Stay, are you not rather hard upon Hartley?' asked Norton, looking slightly amused at her vehemence. 'I know, I can see that he sincerely admires you. It is not perhaps altogether his fault.'

Virginia looked up at him; the wind had brought the colour to her cheeks, there was a suspicion of pleased laughter in her eyes.

'I know what you mean,' she cried, nodding her head, 'though you are too severe to indulge me with even one little piece of harmless flattery.'

'Wait,' he cried, 'if you are so anxious to hear it, do not forestall me. I would have said that I should have thought even worse of Hartley than I do now, if I had not known that such as he had to give must needs be yours.'

'He wants to marry me,' answered Virginia, very coolly. 'His mother wishes it, and he agrees with her; but, as to the rest, I believe that you are mistaken, and I,' smiling, 'ought to know best.'

'Certainly you ought,' he answered, looking relieved, 'and, as you may perhaps remember when you came to me first, I was inclined to agree with you. Since then, I confess it has seemed to me that we must both have been mistaken.'

'I was not mistaken. It is true that I am inexperienced, but yet I knew it quite well.'

'Knew what?' and he looked rather startled.

'I knew quite well that Hartley was not in love with me,' answered Virginia, with great *sang-froid*.

' You seem very confident,' said Norton, with a hardly concealed smile. 'Yet you must know that that is the one subject upon which mistakes are, we are told, inevitable.'

She just glanced at him with an irrepressible question in her eyes, but said nothing.

'What is it that you wish to know?' He had observed and answered the look, but she still remained silent in evident and unusual embarrassment, which raised some curiosity in his mind as to its cause. 'Let me answer the question for you if I am able.'

They had reached the end of the shrubbery walk, and found themselves in front of a decaying orangery. It had long ceased to be kept in repair, as being too old-fashioned in its arrangements for the notice of modern gardeners, yet some flowering shrubs in tubs were still ranged round the walls, and through the festooning creepers overhead a few rays of sunlight fell on the paved floor.

'Shall we not take shelter for a few moments from the wind?' asked Norton, pushing open the door for her to enter.

'Why, it is quite warm, and actually there is a patch of sunshine,' cried Virginia. She drew off her glove and laid her hand on the stone bench, where amidst the rough marks of past years the ray of sunlight lay like a piece of silver dropped among the smaller gold coins of the lichens.

'I fear that it is not strong enough to warm you,' said Norton; he stretched out his hand and took her small chilled fingers into his. 'Why, how cold you are!' he cried, remorsefully. 'I' should not have kept you out. I am afraid you miss your southern skies, and find ours dull and unfriendly.'

'Sometimes,' answered Virginia, evasively, letting her hand lie very contentedly in his. 'You see, until now I have never made a home in England.'

'And Stansfield is not like home. Do you think,' looking at her rather earnestly, ' that it ever could be?'

'Perhaps, at least if . . .'

'If what?'

'If I could have papa here with me,' she answered, in a low voice.

Mr. Stansfield walked a few steps away from her and made no reply. Perhaps it was because some paragraphs in the papers of late had warned him that that topic had better be avoided.

'But when we came in here you had a question to ask me,' he said presently, 'and you have not asked it.'

'A question?'

'Yes, why not ask it? You are not generally afraid to put your thoughts into words.'

Virginia coloured a little, but looked up at him frankly.

'It was only that when you said just now "people tell us in these matters mistakes are inevitable," I wondered if you had found it out for yourself.'

'Mistakes in what matters?' he asked, rather shortly.

'In love and marriage,' answered Virginia, who had recovered her composure.

An irrepressible astonishment held him silent for a moment, but a gleam of amusement in his eyes belied the settled gravity of his speech.

'No, in these matters I have been content to form my judgment upon hearsay. I would strongly advise you to do the same.'

'Then you do not claim to be an experienced adviser,' said Virginia. She had stepped on a ricketty wooden bench, and was balancing herself lightly upon it, as she leaned forward to catch at a spray of straggling clematis above her head.

'Take care; you will fall,' cried Norton, rather irritably.

'No, there you are mistaken,' she answered, springing down with the flower in her hand; 'but, after all, it was hardly worth the trouble. See,' and she held out one or two pallid drooping blossoms.

'Shall I take them as a remembrance of —Stansfield?' asked Norton, laughing, but with an undertone of earnestness.

'I should not like my first gift to be such a poor one,' she answered, fastening the flowers into her own jacket. 'If I were at home at La Vallière, I could offer you something worth having.'

'You would like to give me something?'

'Yes, I both like to give and to receive presents. I see it is not the custom in England, but it seemed so strange to let the New Year pass without one.'

'Which it would have given me the greatest pleasure to receive,' answered Norton, looking serious and regretful. 'Perhaps it is not too late.'

'You mean that you have a birthday coming, perhaps?' suggested Virginia.

'A birthday,' he echoed in surprise, then laughed as her meaning dawned upon him. 'It is a long time since I took any count of my birthdays.'

'I think a great deal of mine. I can remember how I have kept each one of them since I was five years old. Papa,' sighing, 'has been with me the last three years.'

'And he will most probably return

for the next,' said Norton, cheerfully.

'Why, how do you know when that will be?'

'I do not exactly know, yet I feel quite sure that it will not be until the summer. I should imagine that you were born with the roses—some time in June.'

'You are not far wrong; perhaps that is the reason that I love the sun so much. I wish that he would let us see more of him. Look, he is leaving us already.'

For, as they stepped out from their temporary shelter, the last watery gleam of light sank below the bank of clouds upon the horizon, and the land lay before them once more grey, monotonous, and unshadowed.

'I am late already,' said Mr. Stansfield, looking at his watch. 'I ought to have started before now.' But yet he lingered.

'If by any chance you should need a friend,' he said, after a pause. 'If, for instance, Hartley should return . . .'

'But he is not to return till Easter.'

'So Mrs. Stansfield assures me,' he answered, drily. 'Still, in case of that, or any other emergency, to whom should you apply?'

'I really have not considered;' and she laughed softly. 'I do not think that I shall need a champion, though I wish that Jack were at home again to keep me company. But do not look so serious, Mademoiselle Joseph will always be with me, and Lady Mainwaring is a kind old lady; the first time I met her, she told me that she remembered papa, and that I was always to come to her if I needed any advice. I have seen her since that several times, and she has been very good to me. I am not, after all, so friendless.'

'Then good-bye,' he said, and stood still for a moment looking down at her with serious but not melancholy eyes.

'Good-bye! how I hate the word,' cried Virginia, shivering slightly. Then, persistently : ' *When* will you come back ?'

' I cannot say, but Mademoiselle Joseph has my address, and if . . .'

' Norton !' cried a voice behind them in tones of surprised expostulation, ' you will miss the train. You really must learn to be punctual. Roberts had the carriage at the door a quarter-of-an-hour ago.'

Mr. Stansfield turned and surveyed his stepmother with evident displeasure.

She, who rarely ventured out into the garden even on sunny mornings, had now left her chair by the fire, and with a fur cloak only about her shoulders stood shivering in the wind.

' If I miss the four o'clock train, there is always the mail at five-thirty,' said Norton, coldly. ' I think you are unwise to have come out without your bonnet.' He stepped up to the glass door which led on to the terrace, and held it open for her to re-enter the house.

' Yes, it is piercingly cold. You have

been out too long already, Virginia; come in with me!' and she held out her hand to the girl, but Virginia ignored it.

'I am going round to the hall-door to see Mr. Stansfield off,' she remarked. 'I will come in that way.'

Norton looked at once pleased and slightly discomfited as they turned away together.

'Do not go out of your way to vex Mrs. Stansfield,' he said. 'It is never wise to make an enemy.'

'But I never thought of such a thing. What have I done?'

'Nothing—nothing of any consequence,' he answered, hastily; 'and now I must really go, but we will not say good-bye.'

He took her hand for an instant in his, dropped it, and stepped into the carriage. Virginia went slowly up the steps and across the hall to the drawing-room.

'It is very strange that I cannot have a little peace and quiet when it is the only thing I want,' murmured Emmeline, as she came in. 'It is too bad. Here is my train of thought interrupted and my comfort spoilt for the whole afternoon.'

'Why, what is the matter?' asked Virginia, rather absently, as she took off her hat and smoothed her roughened hair.

'Well, you really should try not to put mamma out. It makes me dreadfully uncomfortable, and of course it is not my fault. It is absurd to blame me.'

'But what have I done?' asked Virginia, again, a little impatiently. 'Your mother came out into the garden to speak to your brother about keeping the carriage waiting. If she was angry with anyone, it was with him not with me.'

'Well, it is all the same. I know it will end by making me ill. I was sure when you first arrived that it would make some disturbance.'

'If my presence here makes anyone uncomfortable that is a matter which can be easily remedied,' said Virginia, proudly, and flushing deeply as she spoke. 'I will speak to Mrs. Stansfield. I should be very sorry to remain here.'

'There! now just see how tiresome you are. You take it up in that way on purpose to vex me. I wish you had not such a hot temper, Virginia. You know perfectly well that nothing would vex mamma more than your leaving us, and of course all the blame would be laid upon me.'

'Then what did you mean by what you said just now?' asked Virginia, who was still angry.

'Never mind what I meant. I hate explaining my words, there is nothing so wearisome. We shall do very well now that Norton and Hartley are away. I would much rather have you than be left alone with mamma. I believe you were really sorry the other day when my head

was so bad; and you are not so gloomy as
Norton nor so noisy as Jack.   If you would
not ask so many questions, and try a little
more to please mamma, I should like you
very well.'

Virginia gave her head a little proud
graceful turn, and looked over her shoulder
at her cousin.

'Yes, I understand what you mean,' cried
Emmeline, looking irritated.   'You would
imply that you do not care whether I like
you or not.'

'Not at all,' answered Virginia, who had
quite regained her good temper.   'I wished
you to like me.   When I came here first, I
hoped that you would *all* like me.'

'Good heavens!   What a dangerous
wish!' ejaculated Miss Stansfield.   'You
might as well have thrown a bombshell
into our midst.'

'And why?'

'Why!   For several very good reasons,'
answered Emmeline, oracularly.   'Never

mind, Virginia, it may not be too late, and things may turn out better than I expect. Now pray, don't ask me what I mean, and, above all, don't say anything to mamma about going away. If you are going up-stairs, just ask Martin to bring me down a shawl. The wind is positively whistling round my back. I do not believe the double windows make the least difference or else some horrid sanitary workman has put in a ventilator somewhere. There ought to be a law against ventilation. I am sure it kills off half the invalids in this country. Now that Norton has gone, I am not sure that I shall not take to sitting in the library, only one has to cross that draughty passage to get to it. Still, I think it is the pleasantest room in the house, do not you ?'

'Yes, I have always thought so,' answered Virginia, sighing a little. 'Mrs. Stansfield and Emmeline, Emmeline and Mrs. Stansfield, at breakfast, luncheon, and dinner.

It is not a very cheerful prospect,' she said
to herself, as she went upstairs. 'I shall
stay as much as possible in my little sitting-
room with Mademoiselle Joseph.'

CHAPTER XIV.

'I DON'T like it,' said old Lady Mainwaring. 'I don't like it at all. I think it is bad—altogether bad.'

'My dearest granny, control yourself,' suggested her grandson, young Harry Mainwaring, who sat opposite to her at the breakfast-table. He had a game pie and some potted salmon before him, and looked very happy. 'Why, Stansfield has been a thorn in your side ever since I can remember. First, you used to worry yourself because you thought that the old gentleman was badgered by his wife, and then you imagined that she had managed to get the better of Norton; then you were fearful

lest I should be contaminated by Hartley;
now, if you are going to take up cudgels for
a strange young lady from France, you will
have no peace of mind left.'

'But she is Francis Tennant's daughter,
Harry,' objected the old lady. 'She is not
exactly a stranger. I knew him when he
was one of the handsomest men in London.'

'When, no doubt, he was very attentive
to you,' cried her irreverent grandson.

'I was a widow at the time,' answered
Lady Mainwaring, drawing herself up, 'and
he must be fifteen years or so my junior.'

'That has nothing to do with it. Why,
granny, I am over head and ears in love
with you myself.'

'At any rate it has nothing to do with
the present question. I have not met
Colonel Tennant for years, but I like this
girl Virginia. She has pleasant frank
ways and her father's smile. I like her
and I cannot endure Hartley Stansfield.'

'And he intends to marry the heiress?

Very wise of him. Only I thought she had declined the offer.'

'Precisely, but Mrs. Stansfield never meant the matter to end there. Norton exacts some sort of promise from his brother that he will not interfere with the girl again and on this understanding she agrees to remain at Stansfield. In the meantime Hartley goes off to Dresden for six months to study languages; a very proper arrangement, but unfortunately it lasts only so long as Norton is at home. A fortnight after he had taken his departure, Hartley reappears at Stansfield.'

'And what is he about now?'

'Oh, he is very amiable and cousinly. He has quite forgotten that he ever proposed to her. He has only come home to transact a little business for his mother, and of course the girl has been persuaded that it would be very unreasonable to drive him away from his own home merely because he once forgot himself so far as to fall in

love with her. So it will go on until they
have managed to get her entangled with
him. Why, it is the common talk of the
neighbourhood that they are engaged. She
is placed in a false position already. Mrs.
Stansfield will take good care that she is
not easily extricated from it. As I said
at the beginning, it is bad, altogether bad.'

'Granny!' interposed her grandson, pushing back his plate with an air of satisfaction and replacing it with another. ' Does
Mrs. Miller by any happy chance make the
same excellent marmalade of which you
had a supply last spring? I think it
would help me to pass a correct judgment
on Hartley Stansfield if I might finish my
breakfast.' ·

' A far more important subject to you
than this poor girl's happiness.'

' At least one which concerns me more
nearly,' answered Harry, returning from
the side-table with the marmalade jar.
' But, to say the truth, I wonder why you

should so cordially dislike my old school-
fellow.'

'I despise that type of young man,' said
Lady Mainwaring, emphatically. 'He is
not worse than many others, I daresay.
He has not the courage to do anything
exceptional. But a young fellow with no
backbone of principle, with low tastes and
expensive habits, encumbered with debts
and with no energy to enter upon a profession is not, in my opinion, fit to be
married.'

'I will take good care not to introduce
you to the girl of my heart,' cried young
Harry, coming round to the fireside after
having satisfactorily disposed of muffins
and marmalade.

'Ah! you,' said the old lady, looking up
with unconcealed pride at his tall boyish
figure and his healthy open countenance,
'You are a little different. Everyone has
a weakness for their grandsons.'

'And for their grandmothers. I over-

look a great many serious faults in you,
granny, which I should feel bound to
notice if I saw them in anyone else.'

The old lady laughed as he left the
room, but when he was gone her thoughts
reverted again to Virginia Tennant. 'I
will do something to save her if the opportunity offers,' she said to herself. 'I am
certain that perhaps by no fault of her own
her conduct is likely to be misconstrued.
She is in a false position.'

And Lady Mainwaring was right. Her
observation was keen, her judgments were
just, and in this instance she had not been
mistaken. Mrs. Stansfield had played her
game with caution, and so far with a good
prospect of success. Virginia was in
better spirits; if when one is young, it is
difficult to be always unhappy, it is yet more
difficult to be unceasingly anxious; and
indeed just now there seemed to be less
cause for anxiety. Colonel Tennant had
written cheerfully and spoke of the proba-

bility of an early return to England; and to Virginia in her inexperience the hope burned with a bright if somewhat fitful flame. There were times when her laugh was as free from care and her heart as light as ever; and though Hartley's unexpected return startled her a little, and she could not but recall Mr. Stansfield's forebodings, when she found that he was ready to go back to an easy cousinly footing, she was prepared to meet him half-way. She had not forgiven him, but she could forget if she could not forgive, and she perceived that only two lines of action were open to her : either she must resent his presence in the house, or she must put the past altogether out of sight. The last was the easiest and under the circumstances the pleasantest course to pursue, and she resigned herself to it if not without misgivings at least with a determination to silence them when possible.

'Yet I do not believe that she will

marry him after all,' said Emmeline, who always took a desponding view of matters in general. ' I have always told you, mamma, that she is far too good for Hartley.'

' She will be behaving very badly if she throws him over,' answered Mrs. Stansfield.

' Throws him over! Why, you speak as if they were engaged already.'

'And is not the encouragemeut she is giving him as good as an engagement? There are many things more binding than absolute promises,' answered her mother, loftily.

' So that is your plan of action, is it? Well, mamma, you may be very clever, but I do not believe that you will make it answer. Virginia is inexperienced and incautious but she is very clear-sighted, and you will not succeed in cajoling her . . .'

' Really, Emmeline, I am accustomed to disrespect, but if you mean to insult me . . .'

' Not at all,' answered Miss Stansfield coolly. 'But I did not know what other word to use. I think that you are quite right from your point of view. It would be a very good thing for Hartley to be safely married, and it would be absurd for him to marry without money. By all means help him to marry Virginia if you can, only as I said before I do not believe she is a girl to be easily managed ; you cannot force, and I do not imagine that you will persuade her. You are giving yourself a great deal of trouble,' cried Emmeline, stifling a yawn, ' and to very little purpose.'

'I consider her manner to him most encouraging,' answered her mother ; there is nothing like reiterated assertion, it is apt to impose even upon oneself. ' Yes, most encouraging. He was too precipitate before, but he will know better another time. I am frequently asked if there is not something between them.'

' And of course,' sarcastically, ' you at once reply in the negative ?'

' I am not in their confidence,' answered Mrs. Stansfield, as with a slow and dignified movement she crossed the floor and left the room.

' It is really too bad !' muttered Miss Stansfield to herself, unconsciously repeating old Lady Mainwaring's words. ' If it would not be sure to make a disturbance and destroy our comfort in the house, I should be almost inclined to tell Virginia that they will get her into a scrape. But if I interfere they will be sure to make me uncomfortable, and so I shall let things take their course.' She lighted a candle upon the stand near her, arranged her feet carefully upon a footstool, and took up her book.

It was growing dark outside, and the windows were clouded by the frost. The sun had sunk behind the horizon, leaving a trail of fire along its edge, whilst a few stars already were brightly set in heaven's circlet; but Virginia had not yet returned to the house. She was accustomed to have no companion in her rambles, and it was often a relief to escape from the four walls to the open air, to be free from Mrs. Stansfield's questions and Emmeline's headaches, and to be at liberty to be melancholy and light-hearted at will. She had grown fond of the country; of the woods between whose bare boughs the wintry sunlight glanced pleasantly upon green mosses and yellow bracken; of the brown upturned fields where the plough had been driven over the rich soil and of the close-cropped pastures where the sheep were grazing. She had the pleasure in nature which belongs as of right to one of her children whose heart has not as yet been closed against her influences. To Virginia, as she beheld it, the world was, as at creation, ' very good.'

She came along a narrow field-path this

afternoon on her way towards Stansfield with light untired footsteps. It had been a pleasant afternoon, and she was humming a little French song as she walked. The fading light reminded her that Mademoiselle Joseph would be watching and perhaps anxious and she was hurrying her pace when she became aware that, by so doing, she was coming up with two men taking the same direction as herself, but on the other side of the thick-set hedge at her right. Though, as a rule, perfectly fearless, she was not desirous at this moment of meeting strangers, and she slackened her pace, involuntarily, as she did so, catching some sentences of their conversation.

'Well! I say it is a shame. One ought to have had fair warning, though I guessed what Hartley was after all along. Still, she ought not to have been brought into the neighbourhood unless one was to have had a chance.'

'How do you know it is all up?' said

another voice, which Virginia recognized as
that of a certain young Mr. Denver, whom
Hartley had once brought to Stansfield.

'Why, because he as good as says they
are engaged. Being his cousin has given
him no end of advantages. Mrs. Stansfield
told my mother of it the other day. They
had no business to shut her up as they
have done. It is a regular swindle.'

Virginia stood still, arrested by an over-
powering rush of indignation. Was this
the way in which her name had been
dragged in the dust? Was this the meaning of Hartley's easy cheerfulness and of
his mother's increased complacency? Ah!
Mr. Stansfield had been right. He had
done well to warn her. She waited for a
minute or two until the young men had
passed on, and then, gathering up her
breath, she ran across the strip of common
which lay between her and the park gates.
Once inside them she went more slowly
towards the house. Her first rush of passion

had not subsided, but it was changing into concentrated anger against Mrs. Stansfield and her son; wilfully and of set purpose they had taken advantage of her inexperience, and had abused her confidence, and she . . . she had no friend to take her part; yet even now she was not afraid.

She entered the house and went straight into the drawing-room. Only Emmeline was there still bending over her book.

'Where is your mother?' asked Virginia. Her cousin looked up at her with a fretful astonishment. Her dark cloak was thrown back and one hand tightly clenched its folds; there was a bright colour in her cheeks and a light in her eyes. 'Where is your mother?' she repeated, imperatively.

'Oh! dear, how you do startle one,' cried Miss Stansfield. 'I believe mamma is busy upstairs. What is the matter with you? Why do you want her?'

'Because some one has been telling

falsehoods about me ; and I must find out
who it is.'

'Oh, pray do not make a quarrel here,'
said Emmeline, dismally. 'What does it
signify? people tell untruths every day.
Why should you be so ridiculous as to
take any notice of them. If you go to
mamma now we shall be sure to be quite
uncomfortable all the evening.'

'If you like it better, I will put my
question to you instead,' answered Virginia. She had not taken a seat, but
remained standing slight and erect in front
of her cousin's arm-chair. 'You can
answer me perhaps as well as anyone else.
With whom has the report originated that
I am to marry Hartley?' and a deep flush
of resentment and shame dyed her cheek
as she spoke.

'Was there anyone ever like you for
asking questions?' But Emmeline avoided
the girl's direct glance. 'Does anyone

ever know how or where such reports arise? Of course, if you do not intend it, I will allow that it is annoying; but I cannot see why you should take it so much to heart. If it is not true . . .'

'You know, you know perfectly well that it is not true.'

'Well, and did I not always say so? I am sure you need not quarrel with me about it. I never believed that you would marry him.'

'Yet I hear that Aunt Charlotte, and even your brother has dared to assert . . .'

The door opened and Hartley, smooth and smiling, with a hothouse flower in his brown velveteen jacket, lounged into the room.

'Have you had any news?' he asked, glancing at Virginia. 'I hear that the mail is in.'

She paused a moment before she answered:

'No, I have no news—from Egypt.'

'I wish that you would not come here just now, Hartley,' interposed his sister, hastily. 'Virginia was speaking to me about a private matter.'

'Which it seems is already public property,' said Virginia, coldly. 'Your brother is at liberty to remain and hear what I have to say if he desires it.'

'He does not desire it. I wish you would not be so impetuous, Virginia. I am certain you have put my heart out of its normal state already. I can feel it,' pressing her hand to her side, 'and it is beating quite irregularly. Now, do let Hartley go away and we will talk it over calmly.'

'I have nothing to talk over. I have only a question to ask to which I must have an answer.'

There was a momentary silence. Hartley stood half hesitating between the door and the fire looking doubtfully at Virginia.

'She is very pretty,' he said to himself,

with involuntary admiration. 'No one can
deny that she is extremely pretty. But
one never knows what she may say or do.
She puts one in a great difficulty.'

'May I know what your question is?'
he asked aloud.

'Certainly, if you wish it.'

The flush had faded, leaving her a little
paler than usual; but her look was direct
and unabashed, and her voice was steady
as she stood fronting him, leaning one
hand upon the back of a chair at her
side.

'But I am altogether puzzled,' cried
Hartley, though in truth a misgiving had
crossed his mind which had some faint
resemblance to the reality. 'Yet I am
not afraid. Ask me anything you please.'

'Oh, how rash you both are,' cried
Emmeline, pulling her shawl round her
shoulders and rising from her chair. 'And
yet I warn you that if you remain together
you will repent it.'

But they neither of them made her any answer.

'Well! I shall not stay here to listen to you,' she continued. 'A scene upsets my nerves for a week. Do pray get over anything that is disagreeable as quickly as possible, and remember that dinner is at seven, and mamma will be sure to notice if anything is the matter then. If you were not so selfish, Hartley, you would have listened to me and left the room ten minutes ago.'

CHAPTER XV.

THERE were a few moments of silence. Hartley still looked doubtful He had no desire whatever to quarrel with Virginia, and felt it hard that she should wish to force a quarrel upon him. He had never admired her more, he had never felt at a greater distance from her. It was not her anger, but it was her perfect self-possession, before which he would gladly have beaten a retreat had it been possible; but, as Emmeline closed the drawing-room door behind her, she had cut off his retreat.

'Hartley,' she said at last, turning her eyes upon him. 'I would rather have asked the question of some one else, and yet it is only fair that you should hear it, it is only just that you should have an opportunity to deny the imputation which has been cast upon you.'

He took a step towards her, and seemed about to speak, but she stretched out one hand as if to arrest him.

'No, stay until you have heard what I have to say. Is it true that you have said,—that you have spread a report that I am engaged to you?'

He was prepared for some embarrassment, but he was not prepared for so plain and uncompromising a question, and it was an instance in which a lie could at the most avail but for a time, yet his instinct was to prevaricate.

'I could not have said that,' he answered, forcing a smile, 'because unfortunately—most unfortunately for me—it is not true.'

She sighed a little impatiently.

'No, it is not true, and you knew it,

and yet you allowed it to be believed.'

She paused to give him time for a denial, but he had begun to feel that such a defence must needs break down under her direct gaze. She was impartial as a judge, remorseless as fate, and yet there was no boldness in the blue eyes which regarded him so proudly; at a word, at nothing, he had seen them soften into tears. He had held the little hand, which now lay clenched on the marble chimney-piece, in a warm and friendly clasp. If only he could now escape uncondemned she might be as kind to him again.

'You had no right to allow it to be believed,' continued Virginia. 'You knew that I remained in the house with you only upon one condition, Aunt Charlotte knew it also, and yet now I hear you say that I am to marry you, and she implies that you are right.'

'And, if I thought it, could you blame me?' he asked, quickly. 'Is it wonderful

that my wishes should outrun the reality.
When I returned, and you were once more
willing that we should be friends . . .'

' We were *never* friends,' she interrupted,
with hasty emphasis.

' Well, if you will not have it so now, at
least you allowed me to believe it, and was
it unnatural that I should hope for something more ?   I was not the only one to be
deceived.'   Yet even as he spoke a sense of
shame sent the blood to his face.   The girl
stepped back from him with a movement
not of fear, but of something like
contempt.

'How dare you say so ?' she cried, passionately.   ' Who could have thought it !'
She sat down, and leaned her head upon her
hands, whilst tears which pride forbade to
fall burned in her eyes.   ' You have been
very cruel to me ; you pretended to think
that everything disagreeable was past, and
I was ready to forget it. You purposely
deceived me, and now I shall never forgive

you. I shall never like you again, never as long as I live.'

'Perhaps you may have said something like that before,' suggested Hartley. His discomfiture was so great that his only resource was effrontery. He was in a difficulty, and saw no way of extricating himself from it.

'I did say it before, I said it to your brother. It was he who persuaded me then not to leave the house.'

'What—Norton?'

'Yes, but I ought not to have remained; I should not have trusted you. How have you repaid my trust?'

'I made no promise to you,' answered Hartley, sullenly. 'I have as much right to my place here as Norton.'

'I do not dispute your rights with regard to others; but with regard to me you have none, none whatever.'

He walked away to the window. Her words stung him, and yet he had no answer ready It was terribly unpleasant; Virginia was very angry, and he could not help seeing that she had a right to be angry, only, she need not have carried it to such an extreme. He was very anxious to smooth over matters if possible.

'Perhaps I have been wrong,' he said, coming back and seating himself at a little distance from her. 'But after all, Virginia, you might make a little allowance for me. I am not cruel, I would not be cruel to anyone for the world. I am not capable of it. I hate to see anything suffer. I wished to please you and if I thought first of myself it is only what everyone else does,' cried Hartley, a little plaintively. 'It is you who are hard upon me. I know very well that you do not care for me now; but if what I hoped for were ever to come true...'

'It never will come true.' She lifted her head, and before the indignation of her eyes his own fell.

'Then you will not hear me?' he muttered.

'No, what can you have to say to me? And reproaches are useless. You would not understand them.'

She rose from her chair and moved to leave the room.

'Then what will you do?' he asked, blankly.

'I do not know. I have not thought;' and she passed out without looking at him again.

She went up into her own little sitting-room and threw off her hat and cloak. She was flushed, and drew her breath quickly. The air of the house stifled her. She had been brought up in a purer, freer atmosphere. Mademoiselle Joseph busied herself in folding up in decorous order the things she had flung down; but she was sometimes afraid of questioning Virginia and the girl sat silent, taking no notice; but after a while she looked up and said abruptly,

'I cannot stay at Stansfield, Mademoiselle Joseph.'

Mademoiselle Joseph let her angular figure sink into the depths of an arm-chair and regarded Virginia with a sort of mild and timorous bewilderment.

'And yet I do not know why I should be surprised,' she murmured to herself. 'I expected something of the kind from the first.'

'And what did you expect?' asked Virginia, looking surprised in her turn.

'There were sure to be complications, two young men in the house. It was very unfortunate.'

'It need not have been unfortunate at all,' cried Virginia, opening her eyes. 'But Hartley does not understand the meaning of the word honour, and that is certainly unfortunate. As to the rest, I only wish that Mr. Stansfield were at home.'

'And what could he do? No,' cried the old Frenchwoman with a faint blush. 'If,

as I understand, Mr. Hartley has ventured
to propose marriage to you, it would
be worse, far worse, if his brother were at
home.'

'You always misjudge Mr. Stansfield,'
answered Virginia, 'I think it is his fate
to be misjudged. Perhaps it is his own
fault. When he is in general society, he is
silent and severe. But have you never
observed, mademoiselle, that servants, dogs,
and children are never afraid of him.
They are good judges.'

'And upon what grounds do you, Virginia, suppose yourself equally qualified
to form a judgment?'

'I do not altogether understand him,'
answered Virginia looking thoughtful. 'I
have known him but a short time, and yet
I understand him better than others,
because I like him.'

'You like him!'

'Yes, have I not often said so before,'
cried Virginia, a little impatiently. 'In

this inhospitable land he has been a kind
companion, my only friend.'

'And do you not know that so far from
guiding us aright our likings are very will-
of-the-wisps and lead us astray?'

'I have often heard you say so.' Virginia
leaned forward smiling, and laid one hand
upon the old lady's sleeve. 'Do not blame
yourself, Mademoiselle Joseph, if you see
me sinking in a quagmire. It will have
been entirely, absolutely my own fault.'

'Will that afford me any consolation?'

'It ought to do so. See, I am, for instance, at this moment in a serious difficulty. I am very angry with Aunt
Charlotte and with Hartley, but I am very
glad that I need not be angry with myself.
Still, I do not know what I ought to do.
Papa meant me to stay here,' faltering,
'till he came back. Yet how can I
stay?'

She paused, but Mademoiselle Joseph,
sunk in despairing perplexity, could give

no counsel.　Virginia too remained silent, with her eyes fixed upon the fire.　Then, suddenly lifting them as if a light had broken in upon her :

'Stay, you have Mr. Stansfield's address, you must write and ask him to come back, Mademoiselle Joseph.'

But the governess trembled and hesitated.

'My dear Virginia.　Would it not be an unprecedented proceeding.　What can I say?'

'Say that some difficulties have arisen, and that I should be very much obliged if he could return to Stansfield,' answered Virginia, with composure.　'As for the rest, let us sleep upon our troubles; perhaps they may be dispersed by the morning.'

But, though she spoke cheerfully to re-assure her old companion, she was ill at ease, and she would not go down again that evening but remained upstairs with Mademoiselle Joseph.

The sun was shining brightly between the curtains on the following morning when Virginia awoke, but it was still early. No one but the servants, herself, and Mademoiselle Joseph would be stirring for another two hours, and breakfast was laid for them alone.

'And how did you sleep, my poor dear child?' asked the governess, who had herself passed an unquiet night.

'I went to sleep in search of an inspiration,' answered Virginia, who looked as fresh as the morning, 'and I have found one. I will go and ask old Lady Mainwaring's advice. She has lived a long time in the world and ought to have learnt its wisdom. She has always been kind to me. I will go to her. I can walk over to Hinton.'

Mademoiselle Joseph was relieved. To say the truth, she was sometimes afraid of Virginia's inspirations, but this was a sensible and practical step to which she could take no exception.

Hinton was not three miles off, and it was not yet midday when Virginia was shown into Lady Mainwaring's boudoir. The old lady started visibly as she entered, and thrust aside a newspaper she had been reading, but one glance at the girl's face reassured her. No bad news such as she had dreaded was written there. Her eyes, blue and clear as a pool in which you see a reflection of the summer skies, had no shadow of pain, held no presentiment of sorrow. She received Lady Mainwaring's greeting, which was given with more than usual kindness, without embarrassment, and at once told her story with simple brevity. It was a disagreeable episode in her life. She had no wish to enlarge upon it.

'Yes, I see. I feared it all along. They were determined to draw you into an entanglement with Hartley!' cried the old lady hotly, when she had ended. 'But they shall not attain their purpose. It is very fortunate, my dear, that you were able to defend yourself.'

'It was not quite a question of defence,' said Virginia, laughing a little. 'I acted distinctly on the offensive. I had no need of any deadly weapon, a discharge of blank cartridges would have been sufficient. Yet at the moment I was angry, very angry. I am still very angry when I think of it. I do not see how I can go on living in the same house with Hartley and Aunt Charlotte. I am glad that at least it is not her house.'

'She is the mistress of it.'

'Yes,' answered Virginia, smiling. 'But Mr. Stansfield is the master.'

Old Lady Mainwaring turned with one of her abrupt movements and fixed her keen eyes upon the girl, but no faintest blush rose to Virginia's cheek, no slightest sign of consciousness manifested itself as she sat with her cloak thrown back and her hands clasped round her knees, ready to listen to advice yet reserving to herself her freedom of action.

'Norton Stansfield is away from home,' observed Lady Mainwaring, rather weakly.

'He is, or his mother would never have attempted to deceive me. Hartley would not have dared to insult me,' cried Virginia.

'Why do you say that?'

'Because it is true. He warned me even before he went away. He has been kind to me ever since I came to Stansfield. He understood about . . . about papa. I daresay you think him proud and cold and bad-tempered; but he has been the one person in the house who has cared whether I a stranger were happy or miserable. What is more, Lady Mainwaring, he has been the one person who has been invariably kind and polite to my poor dear Mademoiselle Joseph. I shall always like him for it.'

'And such frank out-spoken liking as this is safer than aversion,' thought the old woman of the world. 'A frank liking is the best of strong-holds against the assaults of love;' and, reassured, she answered cheerfully,

'I have never disliked Norton, though I should not have imagined he was a man to put himself out of his way for other people. His was an unhappy boyhood. It is no wonder that his temper was embittered. His father was completely in Mrs. Stansfield's hands and she always hated Norton. It was an unjust will; you know Norton is only to inherit the property on condition that he makes a home here for Mrs. Stansfield and her children. It is an irritating condition and then there is another yet more important one.' Again she bent her keen gaze, as she spoke, upon Virginia.

'You mean that he is to marry?' asked Virginia. 'Yes, Mademoiselle Joseph told me of that.'

'And what do you think of it?'

'I hope it will not be until I have left Stansfield,' answered Virginia, calmly. 'Mrs. Norton Stansfield might perhaps rob me of my only friend.'

CHAPTER XVI.

'Who is to tell Virginia?' asked Mrs. Stansfield, blankly. Even her well-ordered temperament was shaken; even her mind, as a rule so prudently closed alike against the joys and griefs of others, had received a shock. Upon the table beside her there lay an open newspaper, upon her knees there was outspread a telegram. In shortest, baldest phrase they told the same story. It could not be gainsaid; there could be no mistake; the fact was brought home to them in all its cruel distinctness, and now only one question remained to be answered: 'Who was to tell Virginia?'

Mrs. Stansfield was the centre of a little

group of persons, discordant elements brought together for the moment by the magnetism of one constraining interest.

Norton, still in his rough travelling coat, with a deeper gloom than usual in his dark eyes, stood leaning one arm upon the chimney-piece; Emmeline, roused out of her ordinary languor, sat upright, pale and excited; and, in the background, poor Mademoiselle Joseph was furtively wiping her eyes with a laced pocket-handkerchief, whilst mournful ejaculations and invocations of saints escaped her from time to time in her native tongue.

'Ah, that poor child. She adored her father. It was her one hope to see him return. What a frightful fatality!' she sobbed.

'It must be broken to her.' Mrs. Stansfield had recovered herself sufficiently to speak with some decision. 'She must be prepared. She must not be told the worst all at once.'

'I always told her it was a mistake. She loved him too much. It is miserably unfortunate. Poor Virginia, she will be broken-hearted,' murmured Emmeline; and for once she had forgotten that it made her hysterical to see anyone else cry.

'Where is she?' asked Norton, abruptly.

For a moment it seemed as if no one was inclined to answer that question. Mademoiselle Joseph, absorbed in her lamentations, had hardly heard it, and Mrs. Stansfield, who felt some doubts as to whether Virginia had not gone out from her house upon an indignant impulse never to return, was unwilling to draw attention to her absence or its cause.

'But surely some one must know where she is to be found,' repeated Mr. Stansfield, impatiently.

'Yes, yes, I had a letter, a note, but this terrible news has put it out of my head. I do not know where I have placed it,' cried Mademoiselle Joseph, helplessly searching her pockets. 'Lady Mainwaring has asked her to stay for a few days. She begs of me to join her and says that she is writing to her aunt.'

'I have had no letter;' but even Mrs. Stansfield felt that this was no moment in which to be offended. 'But this will help us over a difficulty. I will write and beg Lady Mainwaring to give her a warning. She must tell her that there is bad news from Egypt and we fear that my brother has been wounded. That will gain time. Then she must bring her back to hear the rest.'

'It will never do to leave her with Lady Mainwaring at this crisis,' thought Mrs. Stansfield, judicious even amidst her perturbation of spirit. 'If she does not return here now, she might never return again.'

It was evening when the sound of wheels driving rapidly up the approach warned those within the house of Virginia's return. Since Lady Mainwaring had given her faltering ambiguous warning the girl had only begged that she might at once return to Stansfield. She had walked restlessly up and down in the gathering darkness before the house until the carriage was brought round, and when once seated in it, with the old lady beside her, she had remained with her face turned slightly away, absolutely motionless, rigidly silent. She had asked no question, not even with her eyes. Once when her companion's tremulous fingers sought hers she found them cold as ice, and pressed them gently in her own, but Virginia did not feel her touch. An awful foreboding, which every moment took a more certain shape, held her in its iron clasp, a fear terrible and unrelenting as death itself froze the warm blood about her heart. As they rapidly traversed the three miles of undulating country which lay between Hinton and Stansfield, her eyes rested with fixed unconsciousness upon the low hedgerows, the clustering trees, the cottage casements through which the firelight glimmered. Some one had said: What was it? He had sent her a letter . . . she had waited so long . . . It had come at last ... The lodge-gates were thrown open and they passed up the familiar approach, and stopped under the portico. Virginia rose trembling to her feet.

Those carriage wheels had struck upon the nerves of several watchers within. Mrs. Stansfield crossed the drawing-room and opened the door into the hall. Emmeline half rose from her chair, but sank down again shivering. For once her mother's self-command had deserted her.

'I cannot,' she muttered. 'Where is Mr. Norton?' to the butler, 'call Mr. Norton.'

'*Ah! ciel!* My poor child,' ejaculated Mademoiselle Joseph, leaning against the wall ready to take Virginia in her arms;

arms so weak and tremulous, and yet the arms of her oldest, perhaps her only friend.

But as Virginia stepped into the hall there was a silence, and she stood still, looking round at them all with blank un-recognising eyes. There was a question to be asked; could no one speak, could no one answer it? . . . It seemed as if they shrank from her colourless face, her dilated gaze; she took a step forward steadily, but still vaguely, like one walking in sleep.

When Mademoiselle Joseph started forward with a half-uttered cry, she put up one hand as if to ward off her nearer approach.

'Tell me,' she says at last, breaking the silence. 'You have something to tell me. Will no one speak?'

But the thrill of anguish in her voice, the blind horror in her eyes, has struck them dumb.

Norton has entered the hall, but he has

taken no step forward. Only a vague distrust of the inadequate support which those about her can give even to her physical weakness, has drawn him there at all. He is well aware of his own powerlessness before the magnitude of her grief; and fears to intrude upon it.

'Oh, God! Will no one tell me?' she repeats.

Once long ago, in school-boy days, he had, in an access of blind fury, freed a fluttering bird from Hartley's torturing fingers. He remembers how it lay warm with its pretty ruffled plumage and beating pulses upon his palm, and how, in a passion of anger and pity, he had wrung its neck. Some such impulse stirs within him now as he thrusts the others aside and takes Virginia's hands in his.

'Come,' he says, rather huskily. 'Come with me.'

The library is empty, and it is there that

he takes her. No one has thought of following them. He has shut the door and they are alone. He has pushed forward a chair, but she takes no notice of it, and remains standing, a slight erect figure, though she is trembling in every limb.

'It was of fever,' he says, breaking the silence a little unsteadily. 'It was a gunshot wound, but fever came on afterwards.'

'When, where?' It would seem as if she can only utter those two words. They sound in her own ears like a voice from afar off.

'In hospital, on the 10th. Friday, the 10th of March . . . It is generally . . . almost always, a painless death.'

Strong as he is, for an instant he averts his eyes from her. He remembers how upon that same hearth she held out the peach to him with smiling eyes; he recalls her childish confidence, her frank

generosity; the mirth of summer, the freshness of the morning had ever belonged
to her. She had been born, as he had said,
with the roses, some time in June. Is it
wonderful that now, as she turns her
delicate death-like face towards him, the
shadow of pain darkens his own?

'Let me see . . . the message,' she says,
gasping a little. Her strength is beginning
to fail. She leans one hand upon the table
to steady herself; her eyes, fixed upon the
column of the paper, look in vain amidst
the blurred lines for the letters of the
beloved name, and Norton watching her
remembers how, kneeling in the firelight,
she had kissed the signature which on
no single page of her life's history will
ever be written for her again. 'I cannot
find it.'

'There are no details . . there is nothing
in the telegram,' he answers, laying it as
he speaks over the paper before her. It
seems to him that anything will be less

terrible to her than the bare printed announcement. 'It is only from your lawyer to Mrs. Stansfield: "*Pray break the news of Colonel Tennant's death to his daughter.*"'

'Yes! but, I . . I do not understand.' For an instant she lifts her eyes, and then as they fall again upon the paper before her, the letters stand out large and distinct, and she knows now that she knew it already.

'*Lieutenant-Colonel Tennant of the —th, in hospital of fever, 10th March.*'

The words repeat themselves over and over again; they are burnt in upon her brain, she cannot escape from them. Then all at once a black cloud obscures her sight; she staggers and falls in a dead faint at Norton's feet.

END OF THE FIRST VOLUME.

LONDON: PRINTED BY DUNCAN MACDONALD, BLENHEIM HOUSE.